AF526789

pratyaksha shukla

A book on Love and Loss

Rising Sun

The Quiet Between Light and Leaving

Pratyaksha Shukla

ISBN: 978-93-343-2980-3

To my sister –
Nurture your soul with love.

Prologue

My mother has always saved the worst version of herself for me.

Hemera frowned, "Writing it out makes it seem. . . real."
Standing up, she closed her notebook with the pen still wedged between the pages. She had recently started journaling, after hearing people constantly raving about it online.

Raising her arms above her head, she stretched with a small pop, her shoulders tense from sitting for hours, writing – tearing the page again and again, she sighed, sure that her dustbin must be overflowing with crushed paper balls. She had never felt older, now thirty-two, a few strands of grey in her dark hair and an ever growing need for exercise to get rid of her lethargy.

Her handwriting was bad.

How do people do it? She was pretty new to social media, having installed a few famous apps recently. Those aesthetic videos with beautiful prose and stickers and dried flowers, colorful pens and what not. Her diary was simple – old with her favorite childhood character on it, the cover used to be bright pink, now a bit faded, yet the pages remained new.

She never did get to use it, always saving it for something better. Something bigger or more exciting.

Her apartment was small – *2 bhk*, her friends called it cosy and colorful. Though she had always remained careful not to splash color on the white walls, the last thing she wanted was for her to get fined or lose her security deposit.

Hemera was a painter. Known enough that her work was displayed in art galleries and functions, other than that, she sold craft and painted Fine Arts online. She earned well enough. In summers when the rest of the flats were filled with the noise of kids all day again, she took summer club classes, teaching drawing to small hands and creative minds.

Unfinished canvases hung across the walls of her art room – the current piece she was working on was still on the easel, most finished ones were wrapped in bubble wrap kept next to her coffee table, her packing supplies laid across the table – the scissor dangerously close to the edge. Hemera picked it up to put it back in the pencil stand.

Her art room was always messy, Mudit used to say it resembled her state of mind. Pencil sketches across the floor, paint on her clothes, brushes in her coffee. She used to laugh at him. *"Suffering looks romantic when it comes to women."* she used to reply.

She had seen suffering, had felt it when she was young and hungry, when she used to tug on her mother's saree asking for attention only for the older woman to ignore her. She had seen how –

Her doorbell rang, musing her out of her thoughts.

When she was younger, she used to drink and smoke like there was no tomorrow, there was an ache in her body – her soul, for something she had yet to find.

Still, she had grown content in herself and her life. She had shoved all those confusing feelings in a box and labeled it *"Don't fucking open"* and had left it rust and decay.

The delivery man left quickly, the letter in her hand felt heavy.

It was sent to her by her mother.

And for the first time in years, she felt that itch again.

1

She was just seven when she lost her father.

Mera was small, her father was always an oppressing force whenever he cared to be around. He used to frown at the sight of her, and she would always clutch her frock a bit tightly when he would scold her for not being first in class. He was a tall man, dark skin and black hair – though he looked younger than his age. He looked like he would not age.

Yes – he was harsh, but he was like the sun, it would get too hot if he was angry but when the sun was soft and the world felt warm, she wanted to stay with him, as long as he smiled and played with her. He would call her, "My Mera." and sneak her chocolates.

She assumed he would live forever.

So, it was a surprise. Car Accident; they said.
She was confused and hurt and her heart was beating too fast as she watched her father being laid across a white sheet before being covered with another. Cotton balls covering his nose – people crying around her.

Her mother wore white too, as she sat next to her; Ma's face was ashen, but she didn't cry. She never did.

If her father was the sun then her mother was. . . she couldn't decide. Her mother was like a rock – unmoving. Or maybe a mountain, she couldn't decide. Ma was harsh, she never gave Mera sweets or played with her. She always stared at her with unblinking eyes and a small frown, but Mera supposed; it was better than her Ma's expressionless face and disinterest whenever she did well.

"Where are they taking papa?" Mera asked, her tone soft and her voice almost a whisper.

Mera still remembers the only time her mother was soft with her. She turned slightly, as if thinking before she spoke. "Hemera, your body is a temple for Bhagwan and you take care of it. Once he is satisfied with your work, he takes you someplace better. You leave your physical vessel and move onto the next world."

She was never called Mera again.

***

They moved from Banaras to Ranchi, to live closer to Ma's family in Jamshedpur. And her mother told her, "From now on, you will live with my family name. Nayantara."

Hemera Nayantara.
She liked her new surname, it made her feel closer to her Ma. It made her feel proud. She doesn't remember her father's anymore.

Hemera packed up her bags to the best that she could and got ready to live in a new city. Truthfully, she did not want to leave her friends but it wasn't like she could argue to stay.

Her friends had been confused, why was she leaving? Her Dadi and other members from her father's family were still in Banaras. But her Ma had said, "They are your father's family, not mine."

She didn't understand why but her mother had slapped her the last time she asked too many questions. She kept her mouth shut.

Hemera made sure to keep her *Slam Book* safe next to her toys in her bag. It held all the information of her friends; names, phone no.s, likes & dislikes and what not. She had gotten it filled during the last day of her class. *Class 1-A* – She was going to miss them, but she knew, when the holidays begin she will get a chance to see them again. Hopefully.

It took the movers almost a week to bring their furniture to their new apartment. She had lived in a big two story house back in Banaras, so moving to an apartment felt suffocating. Her mother had sold most of their furniture and given away her father's clothes, they had only kept the bare minimum for furniture and kitchen appliances.

She couldn't even run in the apartment! It was that small, the moment she began to run, the apartment would end. It was 1 bhk, in an underdeveloped area. The elevator didn't work and all she could see from the balcony was green. Her apartment was on the third floor – 3B. The highest floor available in the building.

There were 3 apartments on each floor, A, B and C. The other two were empty, the building was old and run-down, so Hemera assumed that people avoided it. Her mother had chosen 3B after talking to a pandit about *vastu* and good luck.

There was a small garden with overgrown weeds and an old rusty swing set below the building, next to the ground floor parking. Ma had sold their white maruti suzuki 800 for a few thousand rupees and had just brought her scooty to Ranchi.

Hemera had loved that car.

Her mother got her admission in a small school nearby and took on a teaching position there. She was a dance teacher, trained classically in *kathak*, Ma used to win awards and prizes in every competition she took part in, won every state prize and was going for nationals before her parents found her a husband and then she was married. Then she had Hemera and rest was history.

Now in Ranchi, her mother looked lighter as she picked up an old wooden box from one of the cartons, opening it to reveal a pair of *ghungroos*, sitting on a red velvet cloth.

Hemera wondered if her mother was finally going to smile.

Maybe the clouds of gloom had finally passed.

She was in Class 2-C.

Hemera held the strap of her bag and made a determined face.

Just like the apartment building, her school was old, some windows broken – leaving nothing but the black metal frame which had been repainted over and over again. The benches were old and wooden, with the table attached and no back rest, the walls old and unpainted, some were probably waterlogged and most were dirty.

And after it rained, she could see small red caterpillars crawling across the walls. Students would pick them up on paper airplanes and then throw them out of the windows, giving them a chance to fly.

Her classmates were fine, a lot more boys than girls but it wasn't hard for her to make friends. They were curious, the first few weeks were filled with questions about where she was from, when did she move and how was her old place. There was a difference in the way they spoke hindi but it wasn't difficult for her to catch on.

A few days in, she attended the first assembly, which made her realise that the school had a lot more students than she expected. She stood along the sea of colorful uniforms, far different from the pristine white of her old school and her heart ached, just a little – for her old friends.

While walking back to class, she crossed the dance room and stopped at the sight of her mother dancing elegantly, teaching a group of senior girls. Her Ma had never looked that carefree, she looked beautiful – her long brown hair open; for perhaps the first time she could remember.

Ayra pushed her from behind, "Keep walking or ma'am will scold us."

Hemera wished she could stay to watch.

***

Despite her mother's happy attitude in school, she was still very much the same at home. Hair tied back in a bun, and an expression of disinterest. As if she was looking *through* her.

She tried her best, studied well and tried to help whenever she could. But her mother never uttered a word, never looked at her. She could feel something caving inside her chest, her mind a mess with confusion and stress – was she doing something wrong?

It had been a few months since they moved to Ranchi and she was missing her old friends dearly.

She flipped open her slam book and flipped open Ma's phone, dialing the number of Sadhana, *beep-beep-beep*, she pressed the button. "9-"

"What are you doing?" Her voice harsh, Hemera jumped in shock, turning to face her mother.

"Calling a friend."

"How dare you take my phone without my permission?" Ma snatched her phone back. "And what is that?" she pointed at her slam book.

"I. . . It's my slam book, mummy. Papa got it for me, my friends have filled it with their phone numbers so that I can call them."

"There is no need to call them. You don't live in Banaras, you should not disturb them." and with that, her slam book was gone.

Hemera held tears back.

Why was her Ma always so harsh?

Was she not doing good?

How can she disturb her friends?

She had just wanted to talk to them.

When summer break began, Hemera found out that a Di from Class 9 lived two floors down, someone who had learned kathak from her mother.

She knocked on the door, waiting.

The girl opened the door, looking down at her, asking, “Hi?”

“Hello didi, my name is Hemera. Can you teach me kathak?”

The girl stared at her. Confused. “I am not free daily, I have to study but sure, sometimes? You will have to pay me for it.”

Hemera frowned. “I don’t have money and I can’t ask my ma. I want to learn to surprise her.”

“Come in. Let’s talk.”

Palak Di, as Hemera came to call her, taught her for an hour, sometimes two daily for the whole month of her summer vacation. It was fun, repetitive as she was trying to perfect the basics.

धा धिन धिन धा । धा धिन धिन धा ।
ना तिन तिन ता । ता धिन धिन धा ।

By the end of the summer, Hemera was pretty confident that she was going to make her Ma happy. Maybe finally they can dance together.

She had grown to love kathak.

***

It was her very first heartbreak.

"It hurts her more than it hurts you." The school infirmary nurse stated, applying vaseline over the marks on her face.

Ma had gone mad with anger.

"Stop trying to take everything away from me." She had hissed, ghungroo hitting her face.

But as Hemera sat in the infirmary, staring at the used antiseptic and blood covered cotton balls on the metal tray next to her bed, she couldn't help but wonder. Was she the problem?

Back in class, the questions began. “What happened?” “Does it hurt?” “Who did this?”

Hemera smiled, sad and too old for her age.
“I fell and got hurt.”

I carry my mother’s name
Her blood, sweat and tears
Her dreams and ambitions
Yet, I sit and wait
For just a look of affection
A look of the warmth of the sun
A soft glow on my face

Hemera was 13 the next time they moved.
It was to change apartments, to shift to a better part of town.

The new flat was a shiny 3 bhk with a community pool downstairs, it was a decent sized society with four blocks, nine floors for each building and six apartments on each floor. A small park like garden and security guards at front and back entrances. As far as she remembered, rent was fifteen thousand a month, way less than what you would pay for such a safe and clean society.

Hemera liked it.

And she liked the boy who played football with his friends across the park, despite all the complaints from the old uncles and aunties. *'The kids will ruin our garden!'* they used to sigh and frown.

He was fairly tall – then again everyone was seemingly taller than her 5 '0, still growing; with big eyes and a small mouth, he looked like a mouse, his ears were a bit big too. He was lanky and had really fluffy looking hair. He was also a few years older than her, and it added to the charm.

When she first moved in, she decided to go down and explore the society. *Her new home.* She wore her best frock and tied her hair in a nice ponytail. She sat on the garden swing alone – watching the boys play football; screaming names and creating small dust clouds. It was kinda fun, legs swinging one by one as she waited for someone to come up to her to talk.

Next to the park, she could see two girls walking, they kept walking nearby and whispering about something to each other.

People say the relationships you make as a teen last forever, whether of love or of hate.

Hemera's blood still boils to this day whenever she thinks about those girls. The girls who got close to her and broke her heart. She would have loved to say that her first heartbreak was over some guy who didn't wash his clothes on time. She wished her first heartbreak was a guy. Something she could laugh about with her girl friends.

But fate or whatever deity she screwed over in her past life had made it pretty clear, her major heartbreaks and disappointments will always belong to the women in her life.

It took those girls three days to approach her.

"Sorry, your nose is a bit big-"
"-and it reminded us of a witch."

What an odd thing to say.

Up close, she realised that the girls were twins, both wearing the exact same t-shirt and pair of leggings.

Hemera stared at them blankly. She couldn't help curling into herself. "My name is Hemera, I am new."

"We know. My name's Aanya and she's Aarya." Aanya – the one with shorter hair spoke. "How old are you?" Aarya asked.

"13."

"13? We thought you were 10, the way you dressed." Aarya slapped her hand over Aanya's mouth. "We are 14, turning 15 in a month." Aarya gave her a tight lipped smile.

"If you are 13? Why didn't you come to talk to us?"

"I-"

And wasn't that a question? Hemera wondered. She never had to go and talk to others, people mostly came to her. Maybe that's why she expected the same after moving. It was weird, she felt as if she was being analysed for everything she did. Like a bug under a microscope.

The three of them became fast friends, despite the weird beginnings. Hemera liked them enough. It helped that her mother was happy to see her out of the house in the evenings after school.

She changed schools again when she moved, a better school nearby – which made her Ma seem a bit more elite. Class 7-A.

The school was clean, no broken windows and no disorderly behaviour. Clean monotone uniforms and teachers who spoke english well. It helped that Hemera was good at studies, it made her admission easier. The school had a big football field and a few courts for basketball and badminton. It had a working library and the teachers actually taught painting during the painting period, instead of being sent out of the class to play outside in her previous school.

That was when she finally picked up a paint brush. It was like magic. Her teachers called her a natural – talented and creative. It gave her a huge ego boost.

Her mother had gotten a better job too, but Hemera couldn't – for the life of her – remember what she used to do. All she knew was that her house was bigger, her school flashier and her new pocket money – *five hundred rupees!* – enough for her to buy paint and brushes. She spent days painting on the same sheet of paper: first with white, then with red, watching the colors mix into pink. She liked pink.

She spent nights, hiding in the corner of her new but scant room, using her lamp as a light source to not wake her mother. Using sheets of old checkered maths notebooks and water as a substitute for paint to practice her brush strokes; practicing until the pages got soggy or torn.

But being 13 and liking pink was like committing a hate crime.

She didn't realise back then, but Hemera had slowly stopped leaving the house with frocks on, stopped tying her hair in ponytails or braids. Had bought a lip balm with money she had saved because her Ma had stopped giving her money after she had found her painting a flower reaching for the sun.

She wore her short tops and leggings, hair open and lips glittering pink as she walked downstairs to meet her friends. They walked daily. Always near the park where the boys played football.

Aanya had taught her the ways of growing up, had taught her what to like, how to dress and how to wear the most trendy lip balm.
Aarya had taught her how to wear a pad and how to cheat without getting caught in exams.

Hemera never told them but they both had their eyes on the same guy. Vihaan, a bit of a loser; if they had asked for Hemera's real opinion but being a girl friend meant smiling and squealing and agreeing to her friend's interest and likes.

So, she sat with the twins on the garden swings, despite mosquitos biting through her black leggings. Watching –

"So. . .who do you have a crush on?" Aarya asked. "I don't know his name but," Hemera gestured, trying to keep her movement discrete, "him."

"Him?" Aanya wrinkled her nose, "He's like the biggest loner we've met." she added.

"What's his name?"

"Bhaskar, but everyone just calls him *bhaiya*, he's in 10-B in C.P.S," Aarya shrugged. "He's kinda creepy, he never talks to us."

"And Bhaskar is such an old sounding name." Aanya sighed.

Despite both girls' attempts at discouraging her, Hemera grew excited at the thought of a mysterious boy. It helped that he always gave her a small smile whenever he saw her.

She watched as he kicked the ball towards the makeshift goal area, marked by potted plants.

He glanced towards her and smiled.

***

Over the next two years, she grew taller than her friends and taller than quite a lot of girls in her class. And it wasn't like she was *tall!* Just shy of 5'5. Her hair had gotten long and she loved trying different styles in it. Her hair was now almost as long as her mother's and she loved it.

Despite her mother's nothingness towards her, Hemera still looked up to her. Still looked at the trophies hung across their home's walls. She loved the plants in her balcony, growing in all directions and climbing through the railing. She had grown to love Ranchi and its green peacefulness – the view of trees and tiny houses from her room's window made it fun for her. She would sometimes spend hours in the evening, sitting and watching kids play with pets or cycle on their roofs.

They looked like small specks, dancing under the setting sun.

Her school was going well, she was studying well and despite being with the same class for almost two years now, she couldn't bother to remember the names of most of them. She had made a few friends but it was getting difficult for her to connect with them as the time progressed. They gossiped about guys from other classes and Hemera wasn't social enough to know any of them. When she talked about the guy she liked from her society, they just smiled and nodded – bored from listening to the same story again and again.

Aside from school, she painted whenever she got time to and watched TV when bored. She would go downstairs to walk around with her friends, sometimes they would end up going out to a pani puri stall in walking distance to eat snacks for cheap.

And at nights when her Ma was too tired to move after coming home from her job *again*, she would sneak out on the roof and sit with legs swinging towards the edge. She would sneak her mother's new touch screen phone with her and play English songs.

It was peaceful.

"You know, it's scary to sit like that. You might end up falling."

Hemera shrieked, gripping the solid concrete roof railing for safety. She turned around to face the one who had disturbed her. It was Bhaskar.

"I know." She replied, trying to keep her voice stable – despite her heart beating faster than when her teacher forces her to run during *games period.*

"Don't worry, I like to sit there too. I have been watching you – you know. I live on the seventh floor of block C. I could see you sitting here every few days," he sat on the railing, twisting himself to join her, legs across the edge, "My name is Bhaskar."

"I know, *bhaiya*." Hemera replied again, feeling stupid about calling the guy she liked bhaiya.

"Just Bhaskar."

"Okay. . . I am Hemera."

“I know.” He replied, parroting her words with a small smile.

Hemera smiled back.

“So what are you listening to?”

“English songs.”

“No way– I haven’t met any girl who likes English music too. Who do you like the most?”

“*Evanescence.*”

“I love them.” He smiled again. Hemera liked his smiles.

“Me too. My classmates don’t really know them. Most people here don’t.”

“Same, you’re in 9th?”

“Just started, but my Ma wants me to change schools again, she had me apply for the best,” Hemera rolled her eyes, “the most expensive one in the city. I am waiting for acceptance.”

"Hm, that makes sense. I am in 12th now, I have been studying in the same school since I was 6 and it's boring." He replied.

"But I like the old one."

"Then you shouldn't have applied to another, should've said no." He shrugged.
Hemera smirked, leaning close despite her heart running a mile. "Let me tell you a secret, Bhaskar. . ."

He leaned with a smile, eyes curious.

". . .I filled out all the wrong answers."

He laughed and laughed and Hemera could feel her face heat up.

The next day when she returned from school, her mother was waiting for her at home. It was surprising, her face emotionless as usual. But her eyes – they burned.

"Imagine to my surprise, when I get a call from some aunty from some other flat. . ." She began, her tone soft as she cupped Hemera's face with both hands. ". . . that she saw my daughter on the roof with a boy, late at night." she finished, grip tightening.

"Is that what you have become? A slut?" She hissed the word slut with so much venom that it surprised Hemera. "Are you trying to ruin my life?" she dragged her long nailed fingers across Hemera's face.

It hurt.

"No-"

"I don't care. I don't want to hear anything like that ever again. The last thing I want is for you to run a bright boy's future and drag my name through the mud." She pushed Hemera away. "Get out of my sight."

Hemera's eyes burned with tears as she picked up her bag and ran back to her room.

She couldn't attend school for a week because of the marks on her face.

And when her face finally healed, her Ma left her a new uniform. Hemera frowned, it was for the school – which's entrance exam she had purposefully fucked up on. She wrote everything wrong and she was still selected?

It didn't make sense.

Hemera made the mistake to assume that the marks on her face were enough for punishment but her mother wasn't satisfied.

The next day, she took Hemera to a salon nearby.

"Chop it off."
All Hemera had done was cry.

2

It was her first day in the *'best'* school of Ranchi. She was nervous.

If she considered her previous school strict, this was jail. It was her first day and she had already gotten scolded about her nails being long? – just a thin line of white above her small nails was enough to get scolded. Another teacher cornered her and told her to tie her hair into two pigtails.

Another scolded her for her uniform being slightly small for her even though it was perfectly fine.

To be honest, Hemera had gained a few kgs over the past few months. She had finally picked up cooking, since Ma was usually tired and sleepy and she cooked in bulk, only to chuck most in the fridge. Hemera had grown to hate microwaved meals and wanted to cook by herself.

She had watched a few American chefs cook on TV and they made burgers and pizzas easily. She wanted to try that too.

Her first few tries were burnt or undercooked and disappointing but she was soon learning what old plastic box contained what spice and how to make pasta which she could actually ingest.

Sure, she had gained a bit of weight, but it was for her own good. She didn't look boney anymore. And her uniform was a good fit.

In class, seats were assigned. She sat on the last bench and her partner was a guy – which was surprising because every school she had been in always made sure that girls and boys sat separately.

Her partner was a boy named Mudit – tan skin and wavy hair. Who looked shy as he kept glancing towards her.

She felt another spike of self-consciousness. Her hair was short, making her round face worse and if – *if* the teacher was correct and her uniform was a tighter fit, she must have been looking so bad. She left ugly.

She must have been looking fat.

The day went boring. And every time she even tried to talk to someone, they looked at her weird.

"We don't talk during class." The guy next to her whispered. "Teachers are very strict."

Hemera frowned.

Later she heard rumors about how she was a bitch faced girl, who looked arrogant and that it was weird she joined school late.

Hemera sighed. She hated first impressions.

Back at her house, she threw her uniform in the washing machine and quickly changed into her casuals. She glanced at the clock. 3:37 pm.

She was going to meet Bhaskar on the roof again at 5. He had slipped a note below the entrance of her house – the only way they had been talking once in a while – and she was excited and nervous as she touched the back of her neck. What if he didn't like her hair?

When the clock finally hit 5, she dashed out, locking the door behind her as she walked downstairs – too much in a hurry to use the elevator.

She walked brisk, trying to keep herself hidden as she entered block C; tapping her feet as the elevator slowly crawled to the ninth floor. She snuck a look as the gates opened, sure that no one else had seen her. She climbed the stairs to the roof and smiled as she saw him, leaning next to the wall and waiting for her.

"Come, if we stand near that corner, no one will be able to see us talking."

Hemera smiled in reply.

So that's where she met him and that's where they talked for the next few months.

Soon came winter,
Her classes were going well. She was scoring okay – the course was a bit difficult. She did make friends with another new girl – Akriti, who most people didn't like. It helped that she sat right in front of her so they talked all day. Passed notes when the class was of a strict teacher.
Her seat partner never disturbed her, and whenever she looked at him, he replied with a nervous smile.

At home, her Ma didn't talk to her and she liked it that way. She had slowly grown angry at her mother for acting so badly with her. All her life,

Hemera had only remembered loss. Her heart was like an empty cavity, which should have been filled with love from parents – but it was empty; with space left from a dead father and an absent mother.

It made her question why. Why was her mother so nice to everyone but her? How was she always at fault?

Some part of her always ached and wondered if it was actually her fault.

She still went downstairs to walk with the twins and still painted at home, but most of her time was now spent with Bhaskar on the roof. Hidden and secluded; something which excited her.

It was something special, just for her.

But she was worried, Bhaskar would soon leave for college and she would have her 10th boards. She wondered if they would still stay in touch. 'Maybe I could ask for a phone for my birthday.' Hemera sighed.

It was one of the coldest days of January when Bhaskar stood in front of her and gave her a note. Hemera opened it with trembling hands.

'I think you're kinda cute, be mine :)'

She smiled, staring at the red faced guy and whispered. "Yes!"

***

Hemera had always thought dating was sweet and soft. Like the romance novels she read secretly in school; even though they were for the teachers. She thought – since they both were alike, things will go well.

It started small. Like always.

He questioned her about her day and frowned when she mentioned that she sits with a boy. It took her some time to explain that the teachers choose the seats and that she doesn't even talk to that guy.

Bhaskar calmed down after that.

But the situation grew, after Hemera finally got a phone, after weeks of begging. The latest model – her mother liked to keep up appearances after all.

She loved her phone, loved that she could give her phone number to others and click pictures and listen to music. She could watch videos upon videos of anything she could think of. It was amazing.

Her mother still used an older model, always stating 'Oh, I don't know how to use it.' and despite Hemera trying to teach her, she never budged.

She spent Sunday mornings downstairs, clicking pictures of every flower and fallen leaf, of the sun's glow on the trees and the little birds which flew away even if she tried to be sneaky.

When her boyfriend found out, he got angry again. "Why did you not come to meet me?" he scowled.

"I like spending my time downstairs," She replied. "I don't understand, what is the problem?"

He gripped her wrist tightly. "I will be leaving in three months. I want to spend my remaining time here with you." He leaned close. "Do you understand now?"

Hemera stood still.

"You are very pretty." He smiled, his tense figure relaxing. The tight grip of her wrist was ever-present. He had kissed her then – Hemera hadn't expected it. She didn't like it.

"So now, no more going down to meet anyone else. We will spend our time together, your mum isn't home until 8 anyway."

Bhaskar left with a smile on his face.
Hemera had stood frozen. Without any replies.

She met Bhaskar the next few weeks, ditching her friends and ignoring any calls she got. It was going well; she supposed.

Until she finally downloaded instagram.

She liked insta, she could see who liked what or followed who, most of classmates and even friends from old schools were already on it. It made it easy for her to connect with everyone.

Bhaskar didn't like that she followed boys on it. She frowned and explained that they were just her classmates. And they genuinely were – just classmates.

He had held her wrist tightly again, pulling; nails digging. It was a screaming match.

“If I can’t follow boys, why do *you* follow girls?”

“It’s different!” He had argued.
“How?!”

“It is!”
“Just– *HOW?*”

Her wrist hurt.

“Because I am not a *slut* like you!”

“What the fuck.” Hemera stared at him.
“Have you seen how you look? How you act? Constantly flirting.” He ranted.

Hemera pulled her wrist, eyes blurring. “Get lost.” She turned and ran.

Later she called Aanya, phone between her ear and shoulder as she iced her wrist. She cried as she explained everything.

Aanya had been sympathetic. “It’s okay, Hemera. I am here for you.”

The next day, Hemera woke up to her phone buzzing from texts.

It was Bhaskar.

'I did so much for you and this is how you repay me?'
'You ran away to others the first chance you got.'
'What a bitch.'
'I am breaking up with you.'

The messages went on and on.

A voice message caught her eye, she played it – hesitant.

She could hear her own voice, loud and clear; playing back. She was crying, explaining how she got hurt and how she isn't sure about dating Bhaskar anymore. The very same words she had uttered to Aanya last night.

Bhaskar broke up with her, blocking her across all online platforms.

Aanya and Aarya stopped talking to her, laughing whenever they saw her.

Her heart ached. But it didn't ache for the love of a man she lost, it ached from the betrayal of her friends.

That day, when she went back home. She took down her curtains and hung her old pink ones back.

3

The breakup had hurt. Late at night when she tossed and turned in bed. She cried. How dare he. How was she a slut? Why did people keep calling her a bitch and a slut?

She hated it.

Her performance during Finals had slipped, her mind still reeling from the betrayal from her ex and her friends – and it reflected on her report card; a C.

Hemera couldn't remember the last time she got a C.

Her hands shook under the table as she sat across her class teacher, next to her mother. "She has constantly performed excellently. . ." Her teacher began gently, "But I don't know what happened here." she sighed, disappointed as she handed the report card to her mother.

Her Ma remained impassive.

"I will handle it." She replied before giving her teacher a small smile.

"Don't worry miss," Her teacher smiled, "It's common for teens to lose focus sometimes, she has been doing well and she has great potential. If she does well in 10th then there won't be any problems."

Hemera had liked her teacher, Mrs. Abha.

Mrs. Abha looked at her. "She's very talented. Her paintings are brilliant."

"Paintings?" Her mother tilted her head in confusion. "Yes," her teacher smiled, "She has won every art competition we had this year, it's surprising to see a single student do so. We teachers tried so hard to let other kids win too; you know? It's a competition after all. But every work she submitted blew others out of the water." she laughed.

". . . as I said, great potential."

"Thank you." Her mother replied, unblinking.

"You must be very proud of her."
Her mother just nodded blankly in reply.

Later at home,
"Show me your work."
Her Ma watched as she pulled out her art supplies, papers and other small drawing copies from under her bed.

And Hemera did. Years of work, from the oldest to her current one. All kept safe and tidy.

She barely looked at Hemera's work, before picking up one of her old paintings – a flower reaching for the sun. "No." Hemera whispered softly,

Her Ma's fingers firmly gripped the edges of the paper – delicate. The painting, vibrant and whole, stretched briefly under the tension before giving way with a sharp, unsettling rip. The sound; dry and brittle, like fabric tearing in silence. Letting the paper fall, her mother watched the torn halves flutter slightly in the air before settling like fallen leaves, the destruction final, intimate, and strangely quiet.

"Is this what you spend your time on? How will you get a job?" She frowned. "You got a C. Be glad I didn't slap you right in front of your stupid teacher."

"I want all this out by the time I come back." Her mother pointed at her art supplies and paintings.

And with that, she was gone.

Hemera stood alone in that room for a long time.

She couldn't just throw her passion away. Anger stirred like a storm inside her. She picked her phone up and opened contacts, freezing. 'I don't have anyone I trust enough to store my stuff.' she sighed.

She could ask Akriti but she lived too far away.

Opening insta, she scrolled through her list of followers and stopped.

Mudit.

He lived close, they shared the same bus stop. Without waiting to let her anxiety take over, she texted him.

'Do me a favor. Can you keep my stuff in your house for a few days?'

The reply was instant. 'Yeah sure, all ok?'

Ignoring his question, she asked him for his address.

Shoving all her things as quickly and delicately as she could, she picked up her box and started her walk to Mudit's house.

Standing in front of it, she felt nervous. It was a small two story, with a small stairway outside leading to the first floor next to the black ford eco sport. She opened the front gate, setting her box down as she rang the doorbell labeled 'Dr.Vivek and Family'.

Picking the box back up, she waited.

She could hear the door creaking slightly as it opened and Mudit peered down. He gestured for her to walk up but she shook her head in reply. "I hate stairs." she said loudly.

Mudit smiled, walking down, "Our class is on the fourth floor."

"I know." Her voice was flat, "Keep it safe." She gave her box one last look, hesitant to part with it. But it was awkward with Mudit. They never really talked so Hemera was surprised he was okay with keeping her stuff with him.

He took the box with care. “Yeah. . .um-” he began nervously.

“I should leave.” Hemera replied before turning around and out of the house; not waiting for a reply.

Mudit stood down, box in hand as he watched her walk away.

He sighed.

On her first day of 10th grade, she woke up ten minutes later than expected and had to almost run to catch her bus. The bus was full, new kids taking up seats of seniors who were finally free from school. She glanced around, before spotting Mudit sitting alone – which was surprising, considering every seat was almost full. She sighed, slipping her bag off her shoulders as she walked up to him.

“I like the window seat.” He jumped at her voice, smiling before giving her space to sit inside. She sighed, closing her eyes as the bus started moving; she leaned her head on the window; hearing the hum of the old bus as it slowly took her to school.

She dozed off.

Mudit tapped her on her shoulder, “We have reached.”

Hemera jolted awake, looking at the now empty bus. Mudit stood in front of her, her school bag in his hand and his own over his shoulder. She blushed, embarrassed. “Thanks.” She said as she took her bag back.

“Will we be sitting together again?” He asked as they walked side by side.

“I don’t think so. It depends on our class teacher.”

“Would you like to sit-” He was interrupted by a teacher gesturing at him to walk in a line. He sighed, slowing his pace down so that he could walk behind her.

“Very obedient.” Hemera replied.

“I think the word you were searching for is, disciplined.” He joked. Hemera turned to look at him, staring into his dark eyes;

“Like I said, obedient.”

***

Hemera was nervous. She hadn't done well in finals and she was assigned the very first seat in class. It made cheating difficult too.

Her class teacher had decided that she would sit with Mudit again; with Akriti now two seats behind her. She twirled her pen in hand, flipping the notebook to the very last page so that she could sketch on it.

Her Physics teacher loved to talk, he was an old man with bad eyesight so even if Hemera was finger-painting while sitting so ahead; he wouldn't notice. She started with drawing a circle and then another slightly below it so that she could start to frame her teacher's round face. She started with the jaw, pen gliding with ease as she focused on the curve of his ear.

She had never drawn someone live. It was fun and frustrating – as the man kept moving. She focused on his head, drawing hair with quick sharp lines. She then focused on his forehead and lines on it, the wrinkles next to his eyes and the rectangular glasses on his face. She added his mustache and smiled as she drew two lines for the neck.

It looked good. A bit cartoonish but good.

"Looks spot on." Mudit replied, his eyes on her paper.

"Thanks."

"I was reading this book the other day. . ." her teacher began loudly – right in front of her desk, "and it was about energy, you know? About how energy is never created and nor destroyed. And that got me wondering. . ." he moved towards the blackboard and Hemera sighed.

'The Law of Conservation of Energy.' He wrote big, chalk dust covering his hand.

"When people use energy, it doesn't disappear. . ." He stated. "Now, can anyone tell me what happens to energy?"

Students raised their hands.

He pointed at Akriti.

"Um, it changes forms?"

"Good!" He grinned, "Now. . ."

Hemera turned slightly and gave her friend a thumbs up. Turning back, she finally opened her book and decided to start reading what was being taught.

Later,
She tossed her bag on the sofa, locking the front door behind her. Tying her now-shoulder length hair back, she quickly took her uniform off, throwing it in the washing machine. She filled up her water bottle, picking her towel from the stand so that she could take a shower.

Entering her room, she knew something was amiss. Her pillows had been moved, the bedsheet was unkempt. Her old boxes from under the bed were rearranged. A frown tugged at her lips. 'Ma.' she was sure it was her. Maybe checking to see if she had still kept her paintings.

She unplugged her phone from the charger, checking for messages as she walked into the bathroom.

She liked being home alone. It meant no questions about why she took her phone into her bathroom, despite the amount of times she had said it was to play music. Her mother was always suspicious of her. She treated her like nothing – ignoring for days; and when she did show attention, it was overbearing pestering about every little action, looking at her like she was a criminal.

Hemera preferred her mother's silence.

4

It was one of those dreams where Hemera knew she was dreaming. The sun was shining and she could feel thin fingers running across her long hair. Something which she used to do for herself when she was younger and her hair was longer.

Her gums ached, vision hazy but she could recognize the place she was in – a park she used to visit with her family back in Banaras.

'Why do you always mess things up?' A voice echoed.

The fingers in her hair stilled.

Shadows spilled across the field, slow and creeping; like ink bleeding into old paper. The trees swayed, not with the wind, but with something heavier.

She looked up.

Through her hazed vision, she could see the sky, once soft and blue, had deepened into the color of wet charcoal. Clouds gathered without a sound. No breeze. Just that awful, pressing silence that settles right on her chest. She couldn't breathe.

Hemera opened her mouth to speak, to ask who was there, who had said that – but the words were caught somewhere between her throat and her teeth.

Behind her, the park had vanished. The fingers in her hair were gone too.

And then the voice echoed again, 'Why do you always mess things up?'

Her gums hurt – sharp, sudden, almost electric. She reached up without thinking, brushing her lips. Something small and hard tapped against her fingernail.

A tooth.

It fell into her palm with a sound she felt more than heard.

She gasped. Another one loosened.

Then another.

Panic rose, hot and bitter in her throat. She spit into her hand, white shapes – smooth and familiar pooled with blood.

She tried to scream, but her voice felt faint. She stood frozen.

Alone.

When I was younger, I had dreams.

Dreams I could feel.

And all that I felt was hurt.

Hemera woke up to the sound of her alarm. It was her current favorite song; energetic and fun.

She couldn't help but reach up to touch her mouth. Sighing, 'All are present and strong.' She tapped her tooth. Still, for good measure, Hemera brushed her teeth extra carefully that day.

Walking to her bus stop with a half eaten toast still in her mouth, she looked up at the sky. There were birds circling above. She yearned to go up there, to be like those birds.

"I think I know how you feel." a voice interrupted.

Hemera turned to see Mudit looking at her. "But we don't have time to bird watch, Driver Uncle told me to call you over since you were just standing."

Hemera replied with an awkward sorry. Dropping the last bite to the street dog next to her – who happily munched on it, tail wagging.

"Let's go."

Her class teacher walked in class with a smile.

"Since our annual function is coming, I would suggest you all to opt out this year. You students have your boards coming up soon." Her teacher began, "But if you think you can handle staying late in school and still cover your subjects then be my guest."

"I have the list of events, so if you are interested in any of them, just write your name and submit it with the costume fees mentioned by next monday."

Her school's principal was a bookworm, and it showed on the list of events and functions; all inspired, polished and meaningful.

Hemera's eyes skimmed over the list before she stopped – *Final Play 1: Rabindranath Tagore's* Kabuliwala & *Final Play 2:* Persephone and the Underworld.

Since last year the school had already performed a play based on the Ramayana and another inspired by Shakespeare, they had decided this time to stage a short story and a twisted take on a Greek myth.

Hemera smiled, writing her name down on both. She hadn't read Kabuliwala but she was familiar with the story of Persephone. She decided to read Kabuliwala as soon as she reached home.

Next to her, Mudit kept glancing at her Event list, before writing his name on both plays too.

"Do you know any of the plays?" He asked, "My dad loves reading so I have a lot of hindi books at home. I think I have read Kabuliwala in a Rabindranath Collection of Short stories book."

"I know the myth of Persephone." Hemera replied.

"I thought it was pronounced purse-phone or something."

Hemera snorted, surprised. “No. That's horrible. It’s *puh-seh-fuh-nee.*”

“I think you are wrong.” Mudit smiled.

“It’s way better than your attempt.” Hemera shot back, a grin on her face.

Mudit’s face turned pink before he turned to face the front. Hemera glanced at him, confused at his sudden nervousness. ‘Whatever.’ She turned to the Event list again.

‘2000 rupees entry and costume fee.’

She resisted the urge to bang her head on the table.

Once home, she shrugged the bag off her shoulders, hearing it land with a thud as she rushed into her room. Sitting on her knees, she bent forward – hands searching for her *gullak* under the bed.

Taking the old ceramic pink pig out, she flipped it upside down, opening the circular plastic lid and taking out her money. She kept the gullak aside; the pig still upside down with its tiny feet in the air, to count how much she had saved.

She had two notes of 500 and three of 200.

Hemera sighed, she was short of 400 rupees. Frowning at the idea of asking her Ma for money. 'What can I even say?' She wondered, knowing that her mother will not allow her to participate in something as "silly" as an annual function.

But she really wanted to participate.

She stood up, opening her cupboard for her wallet. "Maybe I have enough?" She murmured. Hemera grew tense, searching again and again.

She couldn't find her wallet. She walked back to the drawing room and opened her bag, sighing with relief at the sight of her rugged leather wallet; edges scuffed from years of use – it had belonged to her dad.

Opening it, she pulled out her final note of 500, leaving a few 50s and 10s.

Hemera smiled.

***

When she placed her Event list in front of her teacher, she looked nervously at his face. Hemera had ended up forging her Ma's signature – not finding the courage to talk to her.

Her teacher; Mr. Gopi smiled. "Good to see you being proactive."

Hemera smiled back, watching as his eyes skimmed over her choice and other details they had to fill.

"Okay, now do you change for 2000?" he asked.

She nodded, "Just 100." she replied, handing the cash over to him. He nodded back, pulling out 100 from the stack he kept on the other side of the table.

"Not many are participating this year from your class." He stated. "Make sure to not skip your studies."

"Yes Sir." Hemera replied, her voice sincere.

Mr. Gopi was a young man, surprisingly bald for his age; he taught History, sometimes slipping from English to Hindi – but always correcting himself as soon as he realised, looking up at the class CCTV.

Hemera found him nice. He was calm and never gave homework.

Sitting down, she looked at Mudit, who said something which made her teacher laugh as he collected money from him.

Mudit turned to her, a small smile on his face as he walked over to sit.

“What did you say?” Hemera couldn’t help but ask.

“That’s a secret.” He replied, surprisingly bold as he winked.

“Probably something stupid.” Akriti rolled her eyes as she walked up to Mr. Gopi, interjecting in their conversation. Hemera nodded in reply.

Mudit stammered, blushing. “I just said that I love history and that’s why I am taking part in the plays cause the stories are of people from the past.”

Hemera looked him up and down. “Very good, buttering Gopi sir up.”

“I was just being nice. . .” he began.

She laughed lightly, “You act like a teacher’s pet. Obedient and a stickler for rules.”

"It helps me escape punishment when I miss homework and gives me a good reputation." Mudit grinned.

"Always plotting, hm?"

Mudit scratched the back of his neck, laughing a bit nervously. "Yeah."

The Annual Function practice began with auditions, students were explained the roles and what lines to act and given a day to practice.

The last two periods of classes were cancelled for practice every day. Students who didn't participate were given a chance to use it as a study or games period; depending on the day.

Hemera looked at the list of roles, and she applied for both – Older Mini from Kabuliwala and Persephone.

There were no lines for older Mini but the students who had applied had to act shy and hesitant; their movements should still be telegraphed in an expressive way. The plot was also edited to make it so that the Kabuliwala – Rahamat had gone to jail for fighting and not for using a knife to stab someone.

For Persephone, the twist was that there was no Hades in their play, most probably to keep the parents from getting angry at the idea of anything romantic or kidnapping related in a school play. The story instead followed Persephone – who longed to explore the world and blossom into an amazing girl and Demeter – who was too scared to let her go.

The principal stated that the play was for parents to understand how children will grow up, have their own opinions and eventually leave the nest and fly away to create their own.

Hemera *loved* the idea.

She stayed up late at night, practicing Persephone's lines again and again in the bathroom, watching her expressions through the mirror.

"No, Mother! I shall not stay here – for I have found love and purpose in the cold, dark roots of my new home. I long to return and nurture the life that waits for me there." she whispered, loud enough to get her emotion across and soft enough to not wake her mother up.

When she walked into the spare dance room, Hemera could hear her heartbeat in her ears.

In front of her were two teachers and the principal. She shot the principal a surprised look. The woman smiled kindly in reply.

“Hemera Nayantara,” she began, “What a beautiful name.”

“Thank you ma'am.” Hemera replied.

“So, please start with Act 4, line 1.” The teacher sitting left to the principal stated, pulling his glasses over his eyes from his head. “I will speak Demeter’s lines,” he added.

Hemera nodded, taking a deep breath in.

Hemera- *Persephone* stepped forward, her voice firm and a determined look on her face.

“*NO Mother!* I shall not stay here – for I have found love and purpose in the cold, dark roots of my new home. I long to return and nurture the life that waits for me there.”

The teacher cleared his throat, looking at the script in front of his hands.

"But you belong to the light with me, Persephone. You are spring, bloom, my blossom, not this shadowed soil you speak of."

Her tone now soft, she smiled sadly. "Light is not just where the sun shines. Sometimes we bloom where no one thinks we can."

"You don't understand the world, child. It's harsh. It'll change you."

'You don't understand the world, Hemera. The world won't wait for your feelings. Grow up and stop crying.' She could hear her mother's voice, words so different from that of Demeter's.

"It already has." Hemera said with a startling realization. She quickly shook herself out from her thoughts, eyes glancing at the script for a second.

Persephone paused, before reaching out gently towards *Demeter.*

"But I am not ruined, Mother. I am growing. I am learning to choose."

And if it was a conversation between Hemera and her mother. . .

Hemera felt bitterness and pain swirl inside her like an inferno – years of neglect and hurt. 'Maybe *you* stopped crying, but don't pretend it made you happy. You've just forgotten what it means to care.' She thought with stark clarity.

She blinked, her eyes misty.

"Now, this part of the script hasn't been shared, I want your genuine reply for this, okay?" The principal smiled, her eyes seemed to glow with. . . *something*.

Hemera nodded, a sudden shyness creeping into her. "Sure, ma'am." she replied, standing straighter.

The teacher flipped the page of his script,

"I was afraid, my child. That if you went I'd lose you forever."

Hemera pondered for a minute, her hand forming into a wrist; she pulled it over her heart.

"But I will return, Mother. Not out of duty. . .but out of love."

Hemera smiled.

The teachers turned to look at the principal.

"Welcome to the play, Persephone." The principal smiled back.

Mudit had gotten the role of Rahamat.

He seemed ecstatic as Hemera relayed her audition for Persephone. She had decided to skip going for the audition of Mini, happy to already secure the role she wanted.

"The first few days, we'll have to revise our scripts and help in creating props and the background set." She cracked her neck – relishing in the satisfying pop. Next to her, Mudit nodded.

The bus jumped over a speedbreaker, going faster than usual.

"I suck at art, I will probably end up destroying something important." He sighed dramatically.

Hemera shrugged, "Not my problem."

She glanced out the window. She was excited to paint again, having volunteered to help paint the background mountains for the set of Kabuliwala.

She felt lighter than before.

The large *previously* white cloth was spread across the floor, edges held down by paintboxes on all edges. Her art teacher had already drawn the mountains and painted the outlines. The only thing Hemera could smell was paint. She dipped her large round brush into the mix of brown paint and some expensive painting medium she hadn't heard about.

The brush moved smoothly, gliding across with surprising ease. She held up her wooden palette with her right hand, multiple shades of brown mixed with white on it – she lightly dipped her brush into one of the small compartments of her palette.

Hemera worked fast, she only had 40 minutes before she had to run across the campus and reach the dance room where her play's practice was held.

"That looks good," her teacher smiled, a streak of green paint on her face, "Just finish that base roughly. I will do the rest. Maybe you can help with the set of Persephone? I am still thinking about what landscape to paint for it." she asked.

Hemera smiled, "Thank you ma'am. I would love to help, I do have some ideas."

The art room bustled with energy and chatter, students grouped together as they worked on different elements. Three ninth graders sat in the corner as they drew and then cut large petals for paper flowers; for a children's music performance.

Some of her classmates were working along on a cardboard train with juniors.

Her seniors worked on carrying in heavy sun boards and big boxes of paints. Two of them solely focused on deciding the costumes and gluing pieces of cotton together to create small clouds.

"Send someone else for this then?" Her teacher asked. "You can go and start drawing on those A1 sun boards for now. We need 6 sun boards together for one scene."

Hemera nodded, almost done with the final brown she needed to add. "Yes Ma'am."

She stood up, keeping the palette down. "Shreya! Amir!" She called out, watching as two students hurried towards her. "Please help ma'am with this, she'll tell you what to do. Don't paint over what I

have done." She ended her statement with a warning.
They both nodded.
She stood up, giving the mountains one last look before she walked over to the pottery section. The sun boards were kept next to the two potter's wheels – out of which one never worked. On one of the wheels sat Mudit, hands effectively working in moving up the earthenware clay.

While being an absolute failure when it comes to art, he was surprisingly great at pottery and other similar crafts. He was making small pots which would then be decorated and painted before being gifted to guests with flowers or a plant in it.

"Very cool." Hemera tilted her head, eyes glued to the moving wheel.

"Thanks!" Mudit gave her a charming smile.

She turned towards the sun boards, moving one with a grunt as she started to rearrange them into the desired grid on the floor. Before she could move the third one, a voice interrupted her.
"Hey, let me help."

Hemera looked up at her senior. "Yeah please." she sighed.

Vidyut was a 12th grader, one of the smartest and best looking in the whole school. A lot of her other friends; Prateechi, Adya – had found him helpful to talk to, when it came to career or studies. Hemera had never talked to him before.

As Hemera helped him move the sun boards, they talked about their roles in their respective plays, Vidyut was playing the role of Mini's father.
Their hands brushed and Hemera smiled before creating distance between them. "Thank you." She replied. "No problem." He gave her a mock salute.

Hemera pulled out a pencil from her pocket and as she leaned down to sit next to the sunboard, she glanced towards Mudit.

Mudit stared at Vidyut's back with narrowed eyes before looking towards her and giving her a small smile.

She sighed, it was too early for her to try to understand what that look meant and why.

Hemera knew how she wanted Persephone's underworld garden to be. She tucked her hair behind her ear and picked up her pencil with a smile.

"It looks beautiful."
Her teacher sighed with content.

Long ivy covered the base of the panels, wild flowers; venus flytraps, pitcher flowers and sunflowers. The rest of the space was marked with areas named according to colors and other similar elements.

"I think if we knew where Persephone would be standing, it would be good to paint the sunflowers facing her." Hemera turned to look at her teacher.

She looked thoughtful, "That's interesting. I will ask our principal."
Hemera nodded, hopeful.

The afternoon sun was burning hot on her skin, Hemera was exhausted after practice, her voice slightly hoarse from speaking loudly. Next to her, Mudit sat oddly quiet.

"What's up with you?" She asked, covering her hands with her school bag so that she could avoid the sun. Mudit sighed in reply.

"It's nothing, anyway. . ." he cleared his throat, "What's going on between you and him?"

"Who?" Hemera furrowed her brows.

"Vidyut."

"What?" Hemera replied, surprised. "Nothing is going on between us. What do you mean?"

Mudit shrugged. "Nothing. Just– you guys seem close."

"Today was the first time I talked to him."

"Oh."

"Um, yeah?"

Mudit laughed, suspiciously sounding relieved.

"What was that about?" Hemera narrowed her eyes.

"Nothing." He smiled coyly.

5

Music was loud, the choir kids were busy – a boy on the Tabla and another on the Harmonium. A girl from another section whose name Hemera never bothered to learn; was playing a hand-painted guitar. Another girl sat with the drums, and the thinnest looking boy she had ever seen was playing the flute. All mixed together into a surprisingly harmonious melody.

They must have practiced very hard.

Mudit took the stage, shabbily clothed – despite the sequence design which made the outfit glitter – with a bag over his shoulder and a few boxes of raisin in his hands as he walked across the stage.

'Kabuliwala, O Kabuliwala!' the third grader who played Mini entered, a big smile on her face.

And Play 1 began.

Hemera watched, eyes glued to the stage from behind the curtains, right after their play, hers would begin. The chief guests were late, which caused the whole event to start late and that snowballed into back-to-back plays; the principal decided to remove the vice principal's speech (which was noted to be in between the plays) and shift it to the very end *if* time was available.

She wondered how angry the vice principal was going to be.

Kabuliwala was a short story, the play being around thirty minutes only.

She watched as Mudit danced around with another student – the one playing as the neighbor, both saying their dialogues about how the neighbor was indebted to Rahamat for a Rampuri shawl.

In a very telegraphed move, Mudit's character acted as if he punched the neighbor on his chest and the neighbor fell down – causing the two characters dressed as police officers to enter the stage to arrest Rahamat.

The story continued, Hemera turned to look towards the audience, the parents and students seemed delighted – or at least Hemera hoped they did, she could only see flashes of camera from the sea of black.

The play ends, with Mudit and Vidyut standing side by side, sad but content as they watch Mini walk away.

Vidyut's character turns to Mudit's, giving him money.

"Return to your daughter in Afghanistan, Rahamat, and may the joy of your reunion bring blessings upon my Mini as well."

The red curtains fell as the audience erupted in applause.

She squared her shoulders, chin held high as she entered the stage.

"Best of Luck." Mudit whispered as he walked down.

Hemera's costume was a sequence dress, in the color of white with fake golden accessories on her arms and neck. She wore a glittery flower crown on her head and stood barefoot.

"And now, let's begin our final performance of the day - Persephone and the Underworld!!"

The audience clapped.

The curtains rose.

And across the sea of black silhouettes, Hemera spotted a familiar face sitting near the front as light turned towards the audience for a split second.

It was her mother.

***

Her play was a success.

As she walked down the stairs of the stage's exit, her hands trembled. Mudit smiled, other students congratulating and cheering about the play with each other. It was a sea of sweaty, energetic students talking – voices overlapping. Hemera found it hard to breathe. She was pretty sure she had seen her mother.

Her vision blurred, she stumbled her way to the main building, entering class 1-E; she walked towards the last bench – picking up her bag, she unzipped the front to take her water bottle out.

Taking a sip, her hands still shaking as she tried to sit; her lungs felt like ice and her throat had thorns, making it hard for her to gulp. She let out a big sigh, trying to compose herself.

"Hemera."

She looked up to see her mother standing with a teacher at the doorway. Her mother looked calm – no visible anger in her eyes or any stiffness across her shoulders.

"Let's go home."

Hemera nodded slowly in reply.

As they walked out of the main building, the way was covered with kachnar trees growing on both sides. Old petals covered the pavement, the way lit with long Victorian-style lamp posts. Near the entrance of the school was the teacher-student parking lot. The function was about to end, and soon, their empty pathway would be filled with parents and children.

Nearing the parking lot, she could see a boy trying to unlock a cycle. Squinting – Hemera noted that it was Mudit.

Hemera hoped that he didn't see her. Ma's grip tightened on her arm, walking faster as the security guard nodded 'good night' at them.

As they waited for their cab, Mudit cycled past them, giving Hemera a smile and a wave.

"Who was that?" Ma asked.

"Just a classmate." Hemera replied, eyes watching his figure slowly getting smaller and smaller.

Her mother frowned.

"Why didn't you tell me about your annual function? Why did I have to find out about it from our neighbors?"

". . . I-"

The cab driver blew the car's horn. He rolled down his window, "Did you book a cab, madam?"

Her mother checked the number plate with the number mentioned on her phone, nodding, "Yes."

"So?" She prompted Hemera, crossing her legs as she looked forward.

Keeping her bag in between her mother and herself, she replied, "I thought you weren't interested."

Ma sighed sharply, turning to face her. "Of course." she muttered.

Hemera froze at her tone.

"I am sorry, ma."

Her mother sighed again, pinching in between her eyes as if she was warding off a headache. "We will talk about this in detail."

Hemera nodded.

"Of course."

The next day in class, everyone kept giving her side glances.

Even her teacher asked 'are you okay?'

Hemera smiled, pushing through her pain as she replied 'I fell down.' again and again.

Many were convinced, but not Mudit.

He cornered her in the empty hallway, most students rushing to get their favored seats on buses. "You did not fall down." He stated flatly. A frown on his face – eyes burning with anger.

It shook Hemera. His eyes had burned with anger *for* her, not *at* her.

"I told you, I fell." she replied, voice equally flat as she brushed past him. He gripped her wrist, softly enough that she could break free.

The skin beneath her eye had turned a dull yellow and green at the edges, with the center a sickly bluish-purple. The swelling had gone down, but the area remained tender and aching.

Just above her cheekbone, where the skin had scraped raw, a rough scab had settled — dark, cracked, and angry-looking. It flaked a little when she washed her face, stinging every time water touched it, she stopped using Face Wash, afraid to feel it sting again.

“Who did this to you?”

Hemera replied with a humourless laugh.

“Doesn’t matter- let’s go, we'll be late for our bus.” She held his hand, fingers intertwined.

Their hands did not break free until they reached the bus.

And as always,

Hemera walked ahead while he followed behind.

6

10th grade ended with a big question on Hemera's mind – what stream to take; Science, Commerce or Humanities. She dm'd her seniors, bugged other students and cornered her teachers in the hallway. Most preferred to follow their parents' instructions – choose science, give JEE or NEET, get into a good college, get married, have kids and settle down – which Hemera had no interest in.

Kids whose parents were into business wanted them to take commerce while parents who were lawyers wanted their children to follow their legacy and become a lawyer too, by taking humanities.

Hemera? She couldn't imagine any of that.

Whenever she thought of her future, she thought of paint. And asking her Ma's opinion was out of the picture – she knew she would be forced to study science, despite liking the idea of humanities more.

Hemera also knew that she had no choice. It helped that Mudit had also taken science.

"So, students can choose their streams now, and after Board's results are out, if they have not scored enough for the subject, they will be moved to the other class." Mr. Gopi gave a consent form to her mother.

"That's fine, I am sure Hemera will score above 85% for science." Her tone betrayed nothing as she pulled out a pen from her purse – despite Hemera's teacher already giving her one.

Next to her mother, Hemera nodded, giving Mr. Gopi a small smile.

"Well. . . I believe that too. So, best of luck." Her teacher replied.

Her Ma nodded, standing up to leave. Hemera hurriedly followed her, slipping a small *'thank you, sir'* to Mr. Gopi.

The session for 11th graders had already begun in early April, while students waited with bated breath for their results to be announced in May.

PCM and PCB sat together for English, Physics and Chemistry;

going into different classes for Maths and Biology during the final period for the day. Hemera ended up with PCM, which was exactly what her mother wanted.

There weren't many girls in Maths, most wanting to be a doctor. Akriti had taken commerce which made it difficult for her to see her friend during the day. Mudit had surprisingly gone with Biology – which didn't have many guys in it.

Hemera's hair was now long enough that she could tie it into two braids – and whenever her teachers weren't looking, she would take a few strands out from the front and keep them like bangs, tucking them behind her ear whenever she saw a teacher looking her way. She found the need for such strict hairstyles stupid and irritating, wishing to instead tie her hair in a ponytail or leave it open. It made her face look prettier; framed with her slightly shorter front hair which she had cut herself.

Despite not growing taller, she had matured and grown in other ways. It made her feel even more awkward and unsure of her body most days. It didn't help that boys created rumors because she had grown curves; it happened to most girls in school, and it was worse for girls who matured early.

After the Bhaskar incident, she had tried to go downstairs to walk and exercise once – only to be brought aside by a group of aunties who walked daily – who had given Hemera some *suggestions.* Suggestions about how she should get her legs waxed cause they were so "clearly" visible from far away. About how she should exercise to lose a bit more weight and not wear lighter colored tops with dark colored bras inside.

Hemera had gone home and begged to get her body hair removed, with her mother just rolling her eyes before tossing her money to go buy a razor; ashamed that her own daughter was called out but not interested in spending money on monthly wax.

She had ended up buying a pink one, which had somehow cost more than the normal blue ones; and she had used that razor until the blades dulled to nothing.

Her classes were tough, the syllabus being stressful and lengthy.

It didn't help that Hemera hated maths.

Her teacher, who hadn't introduced himself so Hemera had named him Robot Sir, droned on and on about *Permutations and Combinations*, his voice flat and mechanical; she wondered what he had been passionate about because it clearly wasn't teaching maths to an uninterested class.

She doodled across the edge of the very last page of her notebook.

A star before she scribbled circles over it – again and again, turning it into a black hole similar to the one she saw in a movie once.

She sighed, glancing up at the clock.

15 minutes remained.

Her eyes fell back to her rough page, pen gliding as she began to sketch.

Walking back to her house from the bus stop, Hemera paused as she noticed something move in her periphery.

A small weak-looking brown puppy jumped into her view with a bark, its whole body shaking with each woof. It looked up at her, wide-eyed and innocent. Hemera crouched down to pick it up, realizing that it was a boy with no mother in sight.

“Hello there.” She smiled, the puppy was silent in her arms; no fear. He felt safe.

Hemera decided to take him home.

He was a bit dirty, probably from rolling around in dirt, paws caked with dried mud. She wondered what to name him, eyes glancing around – Hemera noticed packets of noodles hanging down from a small shop.

‘That’s it!’ She grinned.

She waited patiently in the lift, it was impulsive of her to bring a puppy without asking her mother. She leaned down, gently placing him in between her legs as she opened the door.

“Welcome home, Maggi.”

Maggi zoomed into the apartment, tail wagging as he explored the place with little jumps.

Hemera laughed, watching him walk around so comfortably.

“Let’s get you something to eat.” She decided, opening the fridge and picking out the packet of bread, ‘Can dogs eat bread?’ she wondered as she kept the packet on the drawing room table.

She walked into her room, picking up her phone from the charger to search it on the web.

She sighed. She could feed Maggi bread but she would have to buy dog food as soon as possible.

Hemera walked back into the kitchen, picking up the packet of bread as she went in. She took out an old plastic container from the shelf, tearing up a slice into smaller pieces before she added some water; making sure to not wet the bread completely.

She placed the plastic bowl next to the sofa and watched as Maggi hurried to eat it.

She smiled at him before going into the kitchen to make instant noodles for herself. Making sure to wash her hands properly, unsure if the puppy was sick or just dirty.

She turned on the TV, fork into her mouth as she held her bowl of steaming hot noodles, Hemera knew it wasn't nutritious but she wasn't in the mood to cook.

Hemera noted that the puppy was now sleeping on the carpet.

She switched channels, trying to find something worthwhile to eat with. Deciding to finally settle on the Planet Earth channel. She loved watching documentaries.

After she had eaten, she decided to sit next to Maggi, a wet hand-towel in her hand as she gently wiped his paws. He was so small. Hemera's heart swelled, she could feel it ache as she brushed her hand against his face. She felt a strong urge to protect him. To keep him safe.

Maggi rolled onto his back, seemingly mumbling in his sleep.

Hemera snorted at his funny pose – all paws in air as he slept peacefully.

Her Ma was late.

She worked overtime sometimes so it wasn't uncommon. But Hemera was feeling anxious, worried about her mother's reaction to an unwelcomed guest.

Keys jingled at the doorway, making her stop pacing around the room. She had left Maggi on her bed and locked her room.

Her mother raised an eyebrow at her, closing the door behind as she kept her office bag on the chair next to the entrance. "What?" she asked.

"Ma. . ." Hemera began, taking a deep breath in. "Can we get a pet?"

Her Ma sighed. "I just got home and this is what you are doing. No Hemera, you cannot have a pet."

"But why"

"It's too much work and if it dies early in your care? Besides you have school. No point getting something which will distract you."

"But I will take care of him, I promise!" Hemera frowned.

"Him?" Ma asked.

"I found a puppy today, he was hungry and he chose me."

Her mother sighed again. "Where is he?"

". . . in my room."

Taking her sandals off, her mother walked towards Hemera's room – with Hemera rushing behind her, wringing her hands nervously.

Her Ma opened the door slowly, peering into the room; there sat Maggi, all bundled up and cozy on her bed. She turned to face her, "I want it gone by tomorrow."

"But-" Hemera began.

"He is clearly sick and I don't want the drama that will come when he dies." Her mother frowned, "I don't care how you do it, I want it gone, if I find it home tomorrow, I will get rid of it myself."

Hemera's throat tightened.

"You're heartless," she snapped, voice trembling more with anger than fear. "You don't even care that he's just a baby—cold, alone, and sick. You didn't even ask how I found him."

Her mother turned sharply, her eyes narrowing. "I care more than you think," she said, her tone sharp but quieter now. "You think it's easy? Watching you attach yourself to things that will leave you or die on you? I'm trying to save you from that pain."

"No," Hemera shot back. "You're trying to save yourself from *dealing* with that pain. You said it-*you* don't want the drama. That's not love."

Her mother went still. Her expression unreadable as always, lips pressed into a hard line.

"You think love is keeping something until it breaks you?" she finally asked, voice brittle. "I've seen what pain does. It turns people into ghosts. I won't let that happen to you."

"It already is!" Hemera's voice cracked. "You're so scared of feeling that you've stopped feeling anything at all. I *won't* become like you. Even if it hurts, even if he leaves or dies. I want to love fully. I want to feel everything."

She was shaking, chest rising with shallow breaths. The silence between them hung like static.

Maggi gave a soft whine from the bed.

Hemera turned away, brushing her eyes with her arm. "You can choose not to care, Ma. But I will. I *do.* And I'm not getting rid of him."

Her Ma raised her hand and Hemera flinched.

"I want it gone, I don't care what you say or what you think." Her mother gave her a clipped reply, lowering her hand as she walked away.

She didn’t sleep that night. And as she laid on her bed with Maggi in her arms, watching the rising sun from her window – Hemera promised herself.

To never let anyone or anything decide how much love she was allowed to give.

7

In the end, Maggi lived with her; growing into a beautiful strong boy up until her 12th boards ended.

It was now for Hemera to give competitive exams and get into a college. It was all everyone around her could talk about, it was all everyone asked her.

'So, what now, beta?' The neighborhood aunties cornered her, eyes gleaming with the hope that she'd say something boring or disappointing – something that would make their own children sound better in comparison.

'Still thinking.' was all she replied.

Truthfully, Hemera was still unsure. She wanted to leave her house but she didn't know how she'll take care of Maggi. She wanted a career, a place just for herself where she could paint and dance and sing to her heart's content.

Choosing careers was serious business. Her mother wanted her to become a software engineer – had already started bragging about it to others as if she knew that Hemera will do what she wanted.

She asked Mudit, who said that he was going to be a heart surgeon, having already given NEET and was pretty confident about his results.

Hemera had always wanted to be a painter, which in Indian society meant a loser and a failure.

During the days when others rushed to fill admission forms and give tests to get into the best colleges available, Hemera laid down on her bed; scrolling on her phone. That's when she came across Fine Arts.

It seemed too good to be true, but it held all the elements of a focus on the growing digital landscape while still being "proper" enough to help her earn.

She looked into good colleges and compared costs, finding one in Delhi which fit her mother's budget and offered a bachelor's in three years.

Her mind made up, Hemera booted up her desktop and decided to fill out the admissions form. She looked into requirements and specifications – the college wanted her to submit a portfolio and give an interview for admission along with an aptitude test.

'How to make your portfolio' Hemera clicked on the link, curious.

Hemera rang the doorbell, holding Maggi's leash in hand as she waited. Mudit peered down from his floor, giving her a sense of Deja Vu.

"Hi! Please come up." He smiled.

Hemera shook her head. "The forms close tonight so can't."

Mudit hurried down the stairs, her old art box in hand. It looked surprisingly clean and new. She narrowed her eyes.

"You never visit me and you haven't even seen my house. And this is the first time I have ever seen Maggi!" He moved to pet Maggi.

"The box looks new." Hemera noted, changing the topic as he patted her dog's head.

"Oh. . ." Mudit laughed nervously, "The old one was in a bad condition so I moved your work into another to keep it clean and safe."

Hemera nodded, taking the box. “Tha-”

“Your work is beautiful. . .” Mudit began softly, “You are beautiful.”

Hemera looked at him, caught off guard. “Thank you.” she replied, feeling self-conscious.

“I should leave.” she added, hurriedly, feeling her face heat up as she turned away.

“Bye.”

“. . .bye.” She heard Mudit whisper.

Hemera didn’t look back.

Looking at her old work made Hemera feel strangely nostalgic. As if she was opening up a part of her she hadn’t seen in years; which was true but it still felt weird. Her hands delicately picked up each piece one by one as she laid them across the floor. Mixing those with some of her recent works, she smiled – it seemed that she had a few good enough pieces to submit.

Maggi watched her with a curious tilt of his head from the sofa.

At the bottom of her box was the painting which her Ma had torn up. She joined the pieces, watching her work become whole again.

A portfolio was meant to evoke emotion and show technique. She taped the paper over a black sheet with masking tape, pulling out a black pen from her pencil pouch. She began writing over the taped surface, her phone screen glowing next to it.

It was a quote she had read once – which she had to search again; something along the lines of, *"Perfection is static, and I am in full progress."* by Anaïs Nin.

It felt freeing.

Her mother had taken one look at her hopefulness and squished it like a bug.

"What even is that?" She *scoffed.* "I told you already, you will work towards being a software engineer."

Hemera frowned. "You aren't listening-" her grip tightened around her folder. "It is similar to a software engineer and the college I chose is a reputable one in Delhi."

Ma seemed to perk up at the idea of a 'reputable college in Delhi'.

"Well, I suppose. . ." she sighed tiredly, "I will look into it."

Hemera nodded in reply.
"The admissions closed last night, I have already applied."

Her mother almost smiled at her with something akin to pity. "It's not like your work is good enough, I guess we will have to wait. Meanwhile, I have already chosen a few colleges and paid for admission exams. You should focus on your studies."

She turned around and left the room without a reply, eyes downward.

The next week was spent with Hemera giving entrance exams across cities, in multiple test centers and some online – which was still a relatively new thing. Hemera wondered how they could even tell if someone cheated.

Her remaining time was spent staring at her email inbox with a growing pit of despair in her heart.

It wasn't until Sunday morning that Hemera received the confirmation she had been waiting for. She jumped up from her bed in a silent scream of excitement, covering her mouth as Maggi jumped up, tail wagging.

As her heartbeat calmed down, the feeling of despair came back in full force.

She had to talk to her Ma.

Her mother was sitting on the sofa, newspaper in hand and round glasses in front of her eyes. She peered up at Hemera. "What?"

"I got selected for the interview." Hemera replied, a small smile on her face.

Ma sighed, pushing the glasses up her forehead and folding the newspaper before keeping it on the glass table, "Well that doesn't matter cause, you're not going."

"What? You said if I got selected then I could."

Her mother sighed loudly. "I looked into this Fine Arts thing, it's expensive and worse, it's *useless*."

"I will not do software engineering." Hemera glared.

"You will do as I say, Hemera."

"No. I am going to Delhi and I am going to give my interview."

"You're very overconfident, aren't you?" Ma's gaze hardened, "How will you go? And let's say that you do get selected. . . how will you pay?"

"I-"

"It doesn't matter that if you do end up going for Fine Arts, you will be back home giving me stress again from unemployment. And not to mention, the shame it will bring on my name."

Hemera stammered. "I will manage it myself. I am going and you cannot stop me."

Her mother *laughed*.

"Go." She said, her tone soft. "And when the world breaks you, don't come crawling back to me for help."

Hemera wiped her tears away, a look of determination on her face.

The interview round required students to visit the college on the date they were allotted.

Hemera packed a small suitcase with her clothes and other necessities, shoving all of the cash she had saved in her pocket. She hitched a ride from Mudit on his mother's old scooty – who had been practicing driving so that he could apply for a driver's license. Her suitcase bumped along behind them when the roads were clear, and she lifted it into her lap when traffic grew tight.

As they neared the station, Hemera leaned her head gently against his shoulder, watching the trees blur past.

Stepping down in front of the crowded station, she could hear the announcements loud and clear. "Thank you, Mudit."

Mudit smiled, hands gripping the handle hard with nervousness from driving so far without permission from his parents. "When will I see you?"

Hemera looked at him, as if trying to remember every little detail.

"I don't know."

Mudit smiled sadly, his gaze all knowing.

He reached into his pocket and pulled out a crumpled paper star – something she had taught him to make years ago during a boring geography class. "Keep this," he said, placing it gently in her palm. "In case you forget me." His voice was light, but his eyes held something heavier; something unspoken, tender, and afraid. Hemera closed her fingers around it.

"I will be waiting." He smiled.

Hemera nodded before turning to leave.

She did not turn back.

Hemera had not booked any tickets, being unaware on how to do so. She walked up to the long line of people waiting near the front and waited for her turn.

"How may I help you today?" The lady behind the counter asked.

"I need a ticket to Delhi as soon as possible."

She could hear the keyboard click-click-click away. "There's one that leaves in the next two hours. I can book you on Sleeper Class and there are a few seats available in First AC too."

"How much are both?"

Hemera took out cash from pocket, a giddy feeling as she received her printed ticket. It was her very first train ticket.

As she walked to the platform where her train will come on, she passed a small bookstall. She paused, taking a 50 out from her pocket as she watched him fan himself. "Uncle, can you give me a small diary?" she asked the shopkeeper.

"Here, beta." The shopkeeper smiled. She turned the diary back, checking the price.

"It's 60, I don't have a coin for 10."

"It's fine, girl."

Hemera smiled. "Thank you."

Next she crossed a stall selling sweets and snacks. She paused again. "Two water bottles, please."

She turned around, walking towards the bookstall. She gave one of the bottles to the shopkeeper. "For you."

The shopkeeper smiled, eyes crinkling as he continued to fan himself with an old newspaper.

Hemera waited patiently on platform 8, sitting on the rusty old bench as scrolling on her phone. Her mother would be back home in an hour, and she would read the letter Hemera had left her.

'Will she call?' She wondered.

The train was forty minutes late.

Hemera kept glancing at her notifications. No texts or calls from her mother.

She tried not to feel disappointed; it was expected of her.

Hemera sighed with relief at the sight of her train. The sound of its horn was loud, but the screeching halt — louder. Yet she heard none of it over the beating of her heart.

Her seat no. was 27, the top bunk. She pushed her suitcase under the opposite seat and climbed up the weird shaped ladder; gripping it in fear of falling. It was awkward but she finally settled in, charger in hand as she plugged it on the socket next to her. Despite everything, she didn't sleep that night; her eyes darting with every flicker of movement, afraid that her bag might be stolen, just like it had been once, years ago.

By one in the afternoon, Hemera was a new woman.

Her pink suitcase with old sticker residue rolled and hit the stairs behind her as she climbed her way to platform 1. Delhi was hot, she felt sweaty and exhausted and when she squinted her eyes; Hemera swore she could see heatwaves.

She hailed an auto to a PG near the college. She had found out about it from a college senior she had found online. The senior had told her that they would let her stay a night for free.

Paying the auto driver way more than it should have been, she stumbled her way towards the building.

The guard stopped her at the entrance, just asking her to fill her name in the register. Gripping the blue pen with a sigh as she stood under the fan, Hemera took her sweet time writing. She entered without much hassle, she spotted an older looking woman sitting outside, a tall steel glass of something cold – as she noticed the condensation on the glass; in her hands.

"You must be Hemera?" The older woman smiled.

"Yes." She gave her a polite smile.

"Top floor, third room. The girl just moved out. You can stay the night, and breakfast is before 9."

Hemera nodded her thanks.

Staring at the stairs in front of her,

she let out a loud sigh.

Her room for the next two days was small and clean. The walls were a faded orange and the windows had metal bars over it. It had a single bed with a table and chair next to it. A double door cupboard on the opposite side. The right wall had a door connecting to the balcony which had a clothesline on it.

The walls had marks of previously hung photo frames and posters. The only thing Hemera found odd was the lack of curtains.

The left wall had a door to a small tiled bathroom.

She kept her suitcase down, opening it to take her pyjama and t-shirt out.

Hemera frowned, realizing that she had forgotten her toothbrush. Taking her phone from the charger, she opened the notes app to make a list of necessities she needed. She then went to check how much cash she had.

She'll be turning eighteen soon.

And she had a plan.

8

She waited in the small classroom for her turn, her portfolio gripped tightly in one hand. Next to her, she kept two clay vases which were given to her by Mudit – who had taught her enough about how to mold clay on the wheel that Hemera was confident that she could lie about the vases being her creation. Her other hand fiddled with the paper star.

She had worn a baby pink shirt along with a straight black skirt, which she had stolen from her mother's wardrobe. Her phone's screen lightened up – a message notification from Akriti.

Hemera opened it to find a picture of Maggi on a lawn with a tennis ball in his mouth.

Akriti's cousin; who lived on a pretty big property and had his own backyard, had been kind enough to take care of Maggi in her absence. 'He had always wanted a pet.' Akriti had told her a while back.

'Best of Luck!' Akriti had sent her a text as well. Hemera smiled, replying with a heart emoji.

The Invigilator? Guide? – Hemera wasn't sure – peered into the room, clipboard in hand. "Hemera-" He butchered her name and Hemera winced as she quickly stood up, sliding her phone into her pocket.

"It's *Hemera.*"

He turned around, dismissive. "You're next, follow me."

She nodded in reply.

They walked three rooms down the hall, both vases in her hand and her portfolio folder tucked under her arm.

Her interview was conducted by a man and a woman. The woman had a small smile on her face while the man just looked exhausted.

"Good afternoon, Sir," she nodded at the man before turning to the woman, "and ma'am."

"Please sit."

"So. . . Hemera, why did you choose Fine Arts?" Ma'am began, picking up one of the vases to inspect it. Sir picked up her portfolio, pulling out her work to inspect it.

"I have always-"

"Don't give us a generic answer." Sir sighed. "All I have heard is the same story again and again today, and frankly I am bored. So tell me, why are you here?"

"In this college?" Hemera frowned, confused.

"*No*, why are *you* here?"

Hemera blinked, looking down at her hands before meeting his eyes.

"I'm here because art is the only place I feel like. . . me. It's not a backup plan or a childhood hobby-" She stumbled over her words, "it's how I survive. Art isn't just drawing or color palettes to me. It's storytelling. It's freedom."

"And what if you don't get in here? What other options do you have?" Ma'am asked with an encouraging smile.

"If I don't give this everything I have, I'll always feel like I chose fear over myself."

"Interesting." Sir leaned back on his chair. His eyes on the desk as he picks up her previously-torn painting. "Perfection is static, and I am in full progress." He smiled, exchanging a look with the other interviewer.

"Fine Arts is about expression, and your work speaks for yourself." Ma'am smiled, turning to look at her.

"Well, let's start with this painting of yours."

Hemera smiled.

The next few days went by in a blur. She packed up her bag, thanked the PG warden and left, taking a metro to an affordable hotel near one of the old food hubspots in Old Delhi.

Breakfast was provided by the hotel in the mornings; and in the evenings, when the sun wasn't as harsh, she would wander nearby streets and fill up on cheap roadside snacks – usually spicy chaat or whatever caught her eye.

She had recently gone to Sarojini and bought two tops; one pink and the other being a deeper shade of pink, she was pretty happy with her purchase.

Hemera received her college confirmation letter during her fourteenth day in Delhi, she had turned eighteen a day ago – it being the hottest day of the summer. The sun was harsh and the roads nearby were empty. But for Hemera, it was light at the end of a long tunnel; she closed her eyes as she leaned her head against the window – basking under the sun's warmth.

She was free.

***

but I stitched my soul

out of scraps.

Hemera was back in Ranchi.

And she hated to say it but she missed it. The terrible weather and food – which was mostly her fault but she had limited money – made her previous home of almost a decade feel like heaven with its greenery.

She snuck into her home, sighing with relief that her mother wasn't home. Her train had been late, which had worried her, it was already late in the evening. She had to hurry.

Standing on a small stool, Hemera pulled down an old large suitcase and threw it on her bed. She opened her cupboard and frowned, confusion and fury burning in her mind as it clicked-

All her clothes were gone.

She could feel her vision blurring. 'What the fuck-'

Hemera could distinctly hear the front door open but she couldn't focus.

"What are you doing here?"

She turned with a sharp intake of breath, facing her mother.

"Where is my stuff?" She exhaled sharply.

Her mother stood still at her doorway – she was dressed fancier than usual.

"That doesn't matter since you left. You are not welcome."

"I know. I was never a part of your life," she sneered in reply. "I was back to take my stuff. Where is it?"

"I sold it." Her mother shrugged. "Leave before I call the police."

“How could you do this to me?!” Her voice cracked.

“You have been nothing but a burden on me, do you ever think about that?” Her mother’s voice rose, “Do you think about what you did to me?”

“I hate you.” Hemera replied, her tone surprisingly flat. “All my life, I have tried to please you and you-”
Her mother walked into the room, her stride fast as she raised her hand. Hemera’s face stung, but what hurt more was how *normal* it felt; like she’d been bracing for it her whole life.

“I wish you were never born.”

Hemera picked up the bag she had brought back from Delhi, leaving the ones she had planned to take on the floor.

“I’m not your burden anymore. You’re mine no longer either.” She uttered with a tone of finality.

As she walked out of the house, she saw her mother’s purse on the table near the entrance, picking it up and quickly unzipping it; surprised at the large amount of cash in it.

Hemera pulled all of it, stuffing the money in her pocket. She didn't hesitate.

No guilt, no pause. She had paid for that money a hundred times over. In silence, obedience, and bruises on her body. All she got in return was her empty soul aching for love.

Closing the door with a loud bang, Hemera swore to never come back.

9

Now, I carry only what's mine:

a name,

a dream,

and a bruised kind of hope

that still refuses to die.

Her first semester began in late July.

She had changed her phone number, deleted all her social media, and left her surname blank on the admission form. She had gotten a loan from the bank, and including that with her partial scholarship and free stay in the nearby PG – Hemera felt confident enough.

The only contact she had was Akiti, and only kept it to get updates on Maggi. She had scribbled Mudit's number on the back of one of her sketches, unsure if she would ever use it.

Her class was of one hundred and twenty students, all divided into two batches of sixty each. With her batch two having twenty five boys and thirty five girls; many surprisingly local.

The classroom was cramped, filled with oversized desks, each with a single chair. It seemed like extra seats had been crammed in at the last minute, making the space feel even smaller.

She sat near the front, picking out her seat in the row next to the window. In front of her sat a guy and behind her was another – which she found slightly surprising. Most girls tried to find seats next to each other, mostly leaving the window seat row; instead opting for seats directly below fans.

She had worn the pink top she had recently bought with her baby blue denim skirt. Her hair was tied in a low bun and she had worn plastic pearls in her ears.

When Hemera was two, her father had taken her to get her ears pierced. It was tradition and those gold earrings were one of the few things she remembered getting from her father. It broke her heart when she sold them; but she had no choice. Money was tight and despite what she took from her mother, she needed to have some for emergencies and stationery for college.

The guy in front of her wore a rich cologne. It was strong enough that Hemera could smell it from a table away. He wore a dark shirt with trousers, an expensive looking wrist watch on his right hand.

The professor began with introductions and Hemera found out that his name was Raahi, he was from Delhi and how he chose arts because it sounded fun.

Next was her turn, standing up; Hemera began,

“Hello everyone, my name is Hemera.”

The professor – a sharp looking woman nodded, “And why did you choose fine arts?”

“Because I have always wanted to be a painter.” Hemera replied, feeling slightly inadequate. Most had replied about wanting to work with famous designers, create their own brands or even model.

“Painter? Interesting, moving on-” her professor continued.

Raahi turned to face her, his light brown eyes looked like honey under the morning sun. “Painter huh?” He grinned. “Nice to meet you, Hemera.”

Hemera smiled back in reply. “You too, Raahi.”

She only had three classes daily, Sketching & Drawing, Art History and Sculpture & Clay Modeling for the first month of the semester. Sketching would stretch towards the end of the semester, with the other subjects changing monthly; ranging from Composition & Perspective, Visual Communication Basics and Color theory to Printmaking Basics and Fundamentals of Art.

During break, Hemera stood up and walked towards the girl group – which was huddled together near a corner, all smiles as they introduced themselves to each other.

Hemera smiled, feeling slightly awkward.

But to her surprise, they welcomed her with open arms.

And as she laughed at one of the girl's jokes, she felt lighter than she had in years.

And yet, there was an ache in her chest;

A feeling of hollowness she couldn't fill.

After lunch, she got ready for her Sculpture & Clay Modeling class. The stationery list had mentioned clay tools and an apron. It had ended up being almost five hundred rupees; which made her balk at the expense.

Hemera slipped hers over her head, tightening the straps behind her back.

The class was held in a separate studio, tucked behind the main building, with high ceilings and cement floors smudged with years of dried slip and clay dust. Hemera walked in to find long tables lined with wire tools, sponges, bowls of water, and sacks of terracotta clay.

The shelves had beautiful pots and mini sculptures. Clay made her mind wander to Mudit again; she hadn't talked to him in over a month. He had texted her, asking where she was and how she was doing.

The last text from him was asking if she was okay. He had somehow found out that she ran away and took- *stole* money.

She had grown to like him. It had hurt to leave but she was afraid.

Hemera sighed.

Their instructor, a bearded man with straight hair and a calm, gravelly voice, instructed everyone to sit in silence for the first ten minutes and observe a bust placed on a small rotating platform at the center of the room.

"Today," he began, "you'll make your first impression of a face through coiling, pinching and stacking. Don't think too hard. Let your hands lead."

After a quick demonstration from her instructor, Hemera tore into her clay block.

Her fingers trembled at first, not from nerves but from the overwhelming sense of freedom which hadn't sunk in yet. With every coil she pinched and smoothed, her breath grew steadier. She worked slowly, ignoring the chatter around her, focusing on the gentle drag of the wire tool as she carved out cheekbones – not quite human, but strong.

Next to her, Raahi worked messily, smearing clay across his clothes without realizing. At one point, he leaned toward her.

"Yours looks like it has a story," he murmured, not mocking. His gaze curious and surprisingly intelligent.

Hemera didn't reply.

By the end of the class, her hands were stained orange, her apron caked in dust, and her clay piece stood lopsided but proud. It wasn't perfect; its nose was off-center and one ear drooped like it hadn't heard enough – but it was hers.

As they washed their hands at the basin, the instructor passed by her and said quietly, "You feel with your hands before your head. That's good."

It stayed with her all the way as she walked back to her PG.

The warden sat in front of the entrance again.

"Why are you letting me stay for free?" Hemera whispered.

The woman smiled, "Sometimes, when you look at someone. . . you just know." Taking a sip from her chai as she closed her eyes, "You looked like you needed saving."

Hemera couldn't reply.

She didn't need to.

Lying down on her bed, she let herself grin.

She picked herself up, deciding to arrange her sketches properly in a stack. Picking up the sketch with his number on it.

Every night she kept going back to it, it felt like torture to ignore.

Hemera sighed.

Every time she picked up the sketch with his number, she hesitated. What would she say? That she'd stolen money and run away? That she was finally free but still constantly on edge? No. Mudit had grown into her safety, and she wasn't ready to touch that again.

Mudit had always been her constant – steady, warm, and impossibly kind. He had seen her through silences and storms, never asking for more than she could give. And maybe that's why the thought of calling him felt unbearable. He represented a version of her past she wasn't sure she deserved to reclaim. . . not after everything. He was the one person who had *loved* her without conditions, and now, with her guilt stitched into her freedom and her quiet disappearance, she couldn't bear the idea of tainting that.

Hemera didn't sleep that night.

***

Her first semester ended in December, and as students packed up to leave for their homes, she was going to stay in her PG, which had grown to be her home.

She had become friends with a lot of her batchmates, even the elusive Raahi, whose eyes seemed to always be watching what she was doing.

Raahi wasn't like the boys Hemera had grown up around. He was careless in a way that felt deliberate; like someone who had grown bored of pretending to follow the rules. He wore shirts with expensive yet faded brand logos and carried a sketchbook so messy it looked like chaos. His fingers were always stained with charcoal or paint, and he never seemed to care. But what stood out most was the faint smell of cigarettes that clung to him – like a second skin.

He smoked constantly. In between classes, during lunch breaks, while leaning against the college gate – one hand in his pocket, the other holding a cigarette with a sort of rhythm. At first, Hemera found it off-putting. The smoke, the nonchalance, the way he didn't seem to care about what people thought. But over time, that same indifference started to feel like freedom. Like he had carved out a space in the world where he didn't owe anyone explanations.

And maybe, she envied that.

Their conversations had started casually, shared brushes in the studio, arguments over rock music playing during lunch. But there was something about the way he listened. Raahi had a way of tilting his head, of watching her when she spoke, like her words weren't just sound but something valuable. He never asked too much, never pressed for the past she kept hidden behind smiles.

So, when he told her he wanted to date her, it felt like standing at the edge of something dangerous; but not entirely unwelcome. Raahi didn't know her history, her shame, or the pain she carried in the quietest parts of her. And maybe that's what made the idea of him so tempting.

With him, she could pretend to be someone new.

Standing in front of her PG, a cigarette in hand. Raahi smiled and waved at her. His smoke seemingly disappeared into the foggy morning air.

Hemera shivered slightly, crossing her arms as she tried to sink into her jacket.

December was icy in Delhi, and Hemera didn't own any jackets. She had asked a di from her PG for one, a black puffy jacket which had fit her perfectly.

"Want to try one?" Raahi smirked, flipping his almost empty box towards her. "It helps with the weather."

Hemera shook her head. "I've never-"

"Then try." He nudged the box towards her. When Hemera hesitated again, he gave her the one which he had already lit. His eyes following as she leaned close, lips brushing against his hand.

"Make sure you don't inhale it too quickly or-"

Hemera coughed.

Raahi laughed. "Don't worry, you'll learn."

He flicked the cigarette and crushed it under his shoe.

"Let's go." He grinned, turning to open his car's door for her.

"Where are we going?" Hemera asked.

"You'll see."

They drove around the city for the day, only stopping for food and coffee.

Raahi parked the car near the mall parking. "Let's go shopping!" He jumped.

Hemera laughed lightly, she hadn't gone out the whole semester – which made this outing feel okay. *'As long as I stay within my budget.'* she thought.

They window-shopped through multiple stores before Raahi stopped. He turned to face her, "You *need* to try that."

Hemera looked at the dress on display. It was sheer, black with stars on it.

It looked expensive.

"I don't think I will buy that." She replied. Raahi ignoring her reply – grabbed her hand, pulling her into the store.

"Just try it once, then we'll see."

A tired clerk turned towards them. A dark uniform with a small name tag with the word *'Pihu'* on it.

"That black dress on display." Raahi pointed.

"What size?"

They both turned to face her.

Hemera sighed. ". . . small."

In the dressing room, Hemera stared at herself. The short, midnight black dress was fitted at the waist with a flared hem that stopped just above the knees. The fabric shimmered under the store lights, sheer in parts with tiny silver stars scattered like constellations across the mesh overlay. The neckline was a soft sweetheart shape, with delicate spaghetti straps and a subtle open back. It looked like something meant to be worn under moonlight, bold and beautiful; far from anything Hemera had ever worn.

It was also worth two thousand and five hundred rupees.

Hemera wished she could buy it.

"Come out!" Raahi called out.

A surge of insecurity went through her but she quickly shook it off as she stepped out.

Raahi stared at her, face unreadable for a split second before it broke into a huge grin; slight blush dusting his face. "You look amazing. Let's buy it."

". . . I can't." Hemera replied softly, feeling embarrassed.

Raahi frowned, "Who said you'll be paying?" He grabbed her wrist again, "Let's just get the tag off and your clothes packed."

"Raahi, I can't ask you to pay." Hemera frowned.

"You didn't ask, I offered." Raahi rolled his eyes, "Besides, my parents don't care and this dress is perfect for the party we will attend tonight."

"I-"

"It's fine, Hemera. Let me."

She could feel the eyes of other customers and shop clerks staring at them. Hemera nodded, "Just this once." She replied with a reserved smile.

Raahi nodded, smiling back.

He took her to an expensive club for his friend's party.

Hemera had been hesitant at first. The club pulsed with bass the moment they walked in. The walls lined with velvet, lights flashing violet and gold, and a bar glowing with backlit bottles. Everyone looked like they belonged in a magazine; confident, laughing, and dressed like the world would never end. Hemera stuck close to Raahi, her hand brushing against his as they made their way through the crowd.

He introduced her to a few people – names she couldn't remember, faces that blurred into one another. They looked at her dress and smiled, complimenting her like she was another part of Raahi's aesthetic.

At the bar, he ordered two drinks without asking. The glass was cool in her hand, condensation sliding down her fingers.

"You'll like it," he said, watching her closely.

Hemera took a tentative sip, lips curling at the unfamiliar bitterness. Raahi grinned, throwing back his own drink in one gulp.

"Don't think too much," he said, nudging her gently. "Tonight's just for fun."

Just for fun.

And so, she let go – dancing under hazy lights, laughing louder than she remembered she could, and drinking until the edges of her thoughts began to blur. She wasn't Hemera from a broken home. Not tonight. She was just a girl in a beautiful expensive dress, dancing in a city that didn't care who she was.

In the morning, Hemera woke up with an ache in her head, her body twisted weirdly in the car seat she had fallen asleep in. Last night was a blur but Raahi had brought her back and they had ended up making out in the car before falling asleep – laughing about something she forgot.

Her jacket was draped over her dress to protect her from the cold.

Next to her, Raahi slept soundly in the driver's seat. And despite the spinning, the noise, and the way her dress still smelled like smoke and perfume – what comforted her most was the fact that Raahi hadn't taken advantage of her. He'd stayed close, sure, but never crossed a line.

Hemera smiled softly.

The night had been fun, the hurt in her chest seemingly gone.

10

The next year went by, seasons changed and Hemera turned nineteen.

Her old life, once sharp and suffocating, began to blur at the edges, dissolving into the background like a half-finished painting. Still, it lingered – quiet, watchful, waiting.

The almost two month holiday at the end of year two started with a thought in Hemera's head. She needed a part-time job. Her funds were draining faster than expected, which she blamed mostly, on her growing obsession with smoking, and the nights she gave in to drinks she had sworn off.

But with Raahi, nights were fun, drinks mostly free despite her complaints of paying for it herself. He lived fast, dropping money on frivolous things without a blink of his eyes. His eyes which used to just follow her, now seemed to wander.

They never really started dating, which Hemera had liked – how different it was from her previous relationships; where she had to watch her words and actions, unsure if even one innocent action could lead to chaos. But as the year had progressed, Hemera began to crave for some stability. He would be gone for classes for days – having grown bored of sketching.

He would usually return with tears in his eyes, a bouquet of gerberas or lilies in hand, and the sharp smell of alcohol and antiseptic trailing behind him.

Hemera was getting tired of expecting more.

Sometimes, she'd sit by the window of her room after he left, watching the streetlights flicker. The city felt like a blur – too fast, too loud, too much. There was no label to what they had, no rules to follow or promises to break. Just scattered nights stitched together with smoke, music, his laugh when he wasn't too tired to smile, and the warmth of his hand brushing against hers. It had been freeing, almost addictive – to not be defined by anyone's expectations. But lately, that freedom felt hollow. A silence stretched between them, one she didn't know how to fill.

Some days he would return with laughter in his throat and a stupid story to tell, his pockets lighter and his eyes a little red. Other days, he wouldn't answer calls, wouldn't explain why. Hemera never asked. She wasn't sure she wanted to know. Still, the uncertainty stung.

The PG, which had once felt like her space, now felt cramped and distant. Her room was quiet, filled with the lingering scent of turpentine and smoke, her ashtray too full and her sketchbooks mostly untouched. Even the places they used to frequent – the local cafe, the bars with bad lighting and good music, had begun to lose their charm.

She stopped counting her cigarettes. At first, she had limited herself to one, then three a day then five, then none at all until someone offered her one, and it felt rude to say no. Now, she didn't think before lighting up. The smoke curled around her like a blanket – suffocating and familiar. Each puff wasn't just a craving, but a small surrender. Not just to the addiction, but to the way Raahi lived; fast, reckless, untethered.

Still, she missed the version of him who had smiled like he saw her, *really* saw her. The version who stood with his hands stuffed in his pockets and stared at the stars like they were reachable. She wondered when he had changed, or if he ever really was that version at all.

And when she thought of asking him where he went when he disappeared, what made his hands tremble when he returned, why his eyes always looked tired – she stayed silent.

Because deep down, she already knew.

She hadn't painted in months.

Hemera had found a small cafe which was willing to hire her, it was close and paid okay enough for her to agree. She was going to work as a barista and a cleaner, which made her burn in shame.

The loan she had taken was strictly for college and the money she had saved for emergencies was something she knew not to touch.

Her report card came with a note at the bottom.

'Dear Student, This is to inform you that your current CGPA has fallen below the required threshold of 8.5. Please be advised that maintaining a CGPA of 8.5 or above is mandatory to retain your scholarship. We urge you to take immediate academic corrective measures to avoid revocation of your financial aid.'

She stares at the message in silence, her stomach sinking. The red warning on the screen blurs as tears press against her eyes. Raahi's laughter from last night echoed in her head – the drinks, the smoke, the missed classes. But she doesn't blame him.

She blames herself. *For slipping*. For thinking freedom came without discipline. "What the fuck am I doing?" she whispers, shutting her laptop like it might erase the truth.

She picks up her phone, staring at the notification from Raahi's text.

'i failed i am tired of clg, sorry.'

Hemera knew. "He never cared about any of it," she muttered, feeling bitter and ugly. "He can afford to fail. I can't."

And for the first time, the thought forms fully in her mind: maybe Raahi was never really her escape. Just another form of destruction.

She stumbled slightly as she stood up. Picking up the small cardboard box she had made her dustbin, Hemera began throwing every single half-used cigarette box and hidden bottles into it. Picking out tape from her drawer, she tapes her addiction shut before walking out of the PG to throw it.

Hemera knew she might fall into the allure again, her body already itching for a smoke. She also knew that if she didn't clean up her act, she would fail.

In the beginning, drinking and partying had filled the ache in her heart, made her feel wanted and desired. But the more she spiraled, it wasn't enough. Another drink, maybe another smoke – she used to wonder, maybe just one more and the ache will disappear.

Her feet took her to the nearest stationery store.

"Do you have a 24x36 inch canvas?"

The shopkeeper shook his head, "if you want good quality canvases for a good rate," He gave her a card. "Our main shop has larger canvases, I can ask them to bring a small stock here, or you can visit the shop." He pointed to the address.

Hemera thanked him, staring at the card.

Maybe a trip into the city will be good to calm her.

The shop was in a fairly known area, the price of canvas cheap and the material felt sturdy. Lifting the big canvas, she walked back to the metro station, ignoring all the inquiring eyes of strangers.

As she waited for her metro, an elderly woman walked up to her.

"You look tired, beta. Can I help?"

Hemera turned to face her, she was short; with white hair in a bun and a saree. Her eyes were kind.

"It's fine, thank you, *dadi*."

The woman gave her a smile, eyes crinkling.

And the moment she sat down, the canvas between her thighs – she broke. No fanfare, no noise – just silent, heaving sobs as the crowd stilled around her as if she didn't exist.

That night, she didn't reply to his drunk *'can i come'* text. She stared at her reflection in the mirror for a long time, eyes hollow, lips cracked.

And then, with a strange kind of stillness, she decides, again.

No more distractions.

She picked up a size 18 round brush and dipped it into white. The rim of the bottle was thick with dried paint – a small kind of decay that felt oddly familiar. Evidence of how it had gone untouched for months.

With a stroke right in the middle of the canvas, Hemera began.

The cafe was mostly tidy, she only had to wipe the floors with a mop once in the morning, cleaning cobwebs every week and watering the plants every other day.

The owner was a nice man, who visited the cafe frequently. Who had taken a liking to Hemera.

'You remind me of my daughter.' he had said when he first met her.

Being liked by the owner gave her an advantage, he allowed her to eat without paying and a free coffee every shift she worked. She tried not to misuse it, her diet already being smaller than before – most days she sustained on cigarettes and stale bread.

The owner would sometimes sneak her fruits, which Hemera always smiled about.

As Hemera wiped the counter, her gaze fell to the table at the very end of the room. A woman and her husband sat together, a small girl with them. All of them had smiles on their faces, the daughter sharing a story about her class loudly.

She felt the old familiar itch burn brighter. Hemera turned to look away.

Her third year was going to start in a week. She hadn't smoked or drank in weeks, it was progress. She was doing better, it was going to be okay.

She forced a smile and walked to the sink, rinsing the rag under cold water. Some things still hurt more than they should. But she was earning enough for now – a part-time job that didn't crush her, and new brushes waiting back in her room. That had to count for something.

Hemera took a deep breath, steadying herself. One week left and this time – she'd start on her own terms.

11

Hemera stood at the gates of her PG one last time, a rolled-up canvas tucked under her arm and her suitcase by her side.

She had graduated quietly, and as a thank-you, she had left behind one of her paintings, carefully wrapped and handed to the warden, who had simply nodded and said, “You did good, beta.”

A month ago, she had submitted her final portfolio on a whim to a South Asia Art Exhibition; being one of the winners of the inter-college contest. Last week, the email came: her piece had won. And now, she was flying out of the country for free, with her name on a list of young emerging artists, her work to be exhibited in a gallery she had once read about.

It felt surreal.

But as she rolled her old suitcase behind her into the airport, Hemera smiled to herself. For the first time, the future didn’t terrify her.

It felt earned.

Almost five hours later, she landed in Bangkok.

The weather was warm – bright and tropical. Vastly different from the heat and smell of dust in Delhi.

Throwing her suitcase on one of the single beds in her hotel room, Hemera threw herself on the other one with a slight bounce.

The email she had received stated that she was required to attend the first three days of the exhibition to explain her work. Winning meant a chance to appear in a famous art magazine in India and a five day travel package to Pattaya and Bangkok.

There were a few other winners too, but Hemera hadn't gotten a chance to meet any of them yet.

The next day, Hemera wore her lucky satin shirt, which was a mix of pearly white and pink. She paired it with formal black trousers and heels she had borrowed from a classmate two semesters back which she hadn't been able to return.

The Art and Culture Centre stood tall and bright, its beige spiral walkways winding through sunlight and shadows. Glass panels let in the warmth of the morning, and Hemera could hear the quiet buzz of people and the occasional hum of air conditioning as she stepped in.

Her section was at the far end of the second floor, in a corner softened by warm lighting and muted cream walls, next to the work of a man from Japan. A printed card above her display read:

"The Quiet Between Light and Leaving" – A Series by Hemera __________ (India)

The space left empty for her surname.

Five canvases. Each a fragment of pain, stitched together through color and silence.

The first painting was called *Womb Without Name*, which was a chaotic swirl of reds and greys, with a hollow circle in the center, surrounded by faceless figures. Her brushwork was heavy in this one, textured with frustration. It was the earliest piece she had painted after her first breakdown in college.

The second, *Glass House*, featured a girl seated in a room made entirely of glass, every wall reflecting different expressions of the same face – anger, longing, fear. Through the clear ceiling, stars were painted faintly, as if the sky itself was too distant to offer hope.

The third, *Inheritance*, was more subdued. A grayscale image of two hands – one wrinkled and tired, the other youthful but trembling; reaching for each other but never touching. A tiny thread of red tied around their pinkies was the only color.

The fourth, *The Ache*, was her personal favorite. A hazy figure of a mother holding a child, her eyes blurred out, as if time had worn away her identity. The child in her arms was faceless too, its body almost blending into the mother's. There was warmth here, but it was cracked. A love that had never been allowed to flourish.

The final piece was *Reclamation* — stark and minimal. A bare tree, half in bloom, half burnt. At its base, a girl stood with her back turned, a single white lily in her hand.

As she stood near her display, a woman approached; Thai, middle-aged, eyes warm. She didn't speak, but pointed at *The Ache*, then at her chest, and gave Hemera a small nod with tearful eyes.

And in that moment, Hemera felt it – that this ache she had once thought was hers alone, lived in many others too. And through her work, she had finally let it breathe.

A reporter? Photographer – Hemera assumed – asked her to stand next to each of her pieces, camera aimed as he spoke in a calm way.

“Smile, ma’am.”

Hemera smiled, standing proud.

The next two days went in a blur, Hemera found herself in a large cab with the other winners on their way to Pattaya.

The trip included underwater sea-walk, spa and a visit to local museums and shops.

The air in Pattaya was warm and thick with the scent of salt. As Hemera stepped barefoot onto the sun-soaked sand, the grains stuck between her toes like tiny, stubborn reminders that she was far, far away from the smoke and grey of Delhi. A neat line of palm trees stood tall beside rows of relaxed strangers in plastic chairs, some asleep under wide hats, others laughing over drinks that sparkled in the sunlight.

It was her first time at a beach.

She stood still for a long moment, the blue ocean whispering in front of her, not crashing but humming.

The sky stretched endlessly above, a soft gradient of blue, broken only by the occasional streak of cloud. It made her feel small, in a good way.

Later that evening, when the sun had dipped and left behind a soft golden haze, Hemera sat alone near the water. Her fingers drew slow lines in the sand. No music, no messages, no one calling her back. Just the rise and fall of the tide, and the sound of foreign voices in the distance.

She felt calm. Clean.

As the sky deepened into lavender and the breeze turned gentler, a woman walked along the shoreline, balancing a tray of trinkets and silk pouches. Hemera had tried to avoid most sellers, but this woman's face was kind, eyes sharp with experience. Hemera watched her for a moment, curious. When the woman paused near her, she lifted a string of iridescent; almost violet-black pearls.

"Real," she said simply.

Hemera ran her fingers over them. They weren't flawless; some were misshapen and uneven in colour but they glowed faintly under the last ray of sunlight. She didn't ask for a price. She just nodded.

The woman smiled and carefully placed the bracelet in a small cloth bag.

Later, back in her hotel room, Hemera sat on the edge of the bed, the pearls in her palm. Rough. Uneven. Real. She didn't wear them. Not yet.

She just held them close, letting their quiet weight remind her of who she was becoming.

The next day, she went underwater sea-walking with the other winners – who Hemera was growing to like.

The instructor was an Indian guy named Manav, who said that his love for adventure had gotten him here.

The ocean floor felt otherworldly. Even with the bulky twenty kg helmet pressed around her head and the quiet rush of bubbles filling her ears, Hemera felt strangely at peace. Tiny fish darted past, weaving through coral like flashes of living light, their scales catching what little sun pierced under.

She reached out instinctively, hand brushing against the cool bar fixed for balance. It was surreal – the pressure of the water around her, the muffled silence, the slow rhythm of breath. She turned to one of the other winners, who flashed a peace sign and laughed, though no sound came. Hemera did the same, laughing brighter than she had ever before.

Later, as she changed into dry clothes, sand stuck between her toes and hair curling at the edges, she looked at herself in the mirror of the beach shack and smiled – the kind that starts in the eyes.

Coming back from Thailand, Hemera's first trip from Delhi was to Ranchi to meet Maggi again.

Maggi had grown happier and stronger, and despite Hemera's intentions of taking him with her to her new flat in Lucknow, she left him with her friend's cousin, who had grown to love Maggi like his own.

On her last morning in Ranchi, Hemera sat on the balcony steps, Maggi curled beside her, his head resting on her thigh. His fur had grown thicker, and he no longer flinched at sudden sounds. She scratched behind his ears, feeling that familiar tug in her chest. *Love*, she thought, wasn't always in the holding on. Sometimes, it was in the letting go; in trusting that someone else could give what you once did. Maggi nuzzled closer, as if sensing the goodbye.

Hemera whispered a promise she hoped he wouldn't need to understand: *You'll always belong to my heart, even if I can't be in your world each day.* And then, with tears in her eyes and mud still on her shoes, she stood up and walked away.

Jet-lagged, Hemera began to unpack her bare essentials into her new 1 bhk. It was one of those flats which already had furniture, and it was a ten minute walk to the Design Studio she had gotten a job as a creative assistant in.

She was excited, her checklist of things she needed to complete to be free had grown shorter as the years went by. Only two on her list remained, one, to pay her rent and two, to finally call her friend.

12

Despite her plan to contact Mudit as soon as possible again, another year went by. Now, twenty four nearing twenty five, Hemera wondered if it was appropriate to contact him again. What if he didn't like her?

Her recent painting on *love and loss* was getting a feature in an exhibition in Mumbai, and she was invited to talk about it on a podcast with an art enthusiast.

Hemera waited for her luggage near bag aisle 7, picking up her new creme suitcase with a sigh. Following the signs, she hopped on an escalator towards the exit. The glass door opened with a small beep, blasting her face with humid air.

Before she could walk out, a hand tapped her shoulder.

Hemera turned slowly, already rehearsing a polite smile to offer another stranger – but stopped short.

It was Mudit.

Older now, leaner. His face had lost some of its roundness, jaw more defined. There was a faint scar above his right eyebrow, jagged but healed and his white shirt had a pale smear of something along the wrist – maybe airport coffee or chutney from one of those cling-wrapped stale triangle sandwiches they sell at every terminal.

But his eyes; those eyes hadn't changed. Still the same warm, steady brown.

"Hey," he said, soft, almost unsure. "It's you."

Hemera blinked. Her mouth parted slightly, breath caught between disbelief and something quieter – something that had waited years.

"Mudit?" she said. It felt unreal to say his name out loud again.

He let out a laugh, low and nervous. "I wasn't sure. I thought- maybe I was wrong. Your hair's longer and lighter, and your ears have many piercings. You look…"

He didn't finish the sentence, and that was fine with her. There was too much time, too much silence between them to fill in one greeting.

She noticed the slight sheen on his forehead, the way his bag was slung carelessly over one shoulder. He looked like he'd run or maybe hesitated too long, then decided to follow her anyway.

"My friends are just–" he gestured vaguely behind him, "they're getting water or something. I saw you from the escalator. Couldn't believe it."

Hemera nodded slowly, heartbeat in her throat. He was taller than she remembered – or maybe it was the shoes – but his presence felt the same. Gentle.

And for the first time in a long time, she smiled like the past hadn't broken her completely.

"Yeah. . . I am just here for an exhibition, I lost all my contacts so-" she started to explain.

Mudit shrugged lightly, smiling. "It's okay. I saw your other exhibition in the magazine, beautiful work."

"Thank you. . . I should go now." Hemera replied, giving her wrist watch a quick glance.

"Here-" He pulled out his phone. "Give me your number."

Her hands shook slightly, "Sure." She smiled.

Leaving Mudit the second time after seeing him again left weird.

He had tried to give her a goodbye hug while she tried to shake his hand. Both had ended up laughing at each other's uncertainty before finally hugging a bye.

Her cab was stuck in traffic, the driver playing – what she assumed to be marathi songs, she sighed. Feeling a headache building behind her eyes from the continuous horn.

Seeing Mudit again had struck a thought in her mind, which had left her pleasantly surprised. She hadn't thought about her mother in a very long time.

She had finally outgrown the box she was born in.

***

It took Mudit a month before he texted her.

'Hiii its me'

A few minutes later, he texted again. *'Mudit'*

Hemera laughed lightly, already picturing him nervous and shy.

'Hi Doc.' she replied.

'My holidayz start soon so lets meet again??'

She snorted at his punctuation. *'Sure, come to lucknow?'*

'YES'

Hemera did not own a car, nor a scooty; which meant that Mudit had ended up taking a cab to her apartment.

The doorbell rang and Hemera jumped in excitement before standing still.

She opened the door with a smile.

The room was dimly lit a soft yellow by a lamp, casting a warm pool of light into the corners. Two mugs of untouched chai sat on the table, cooling slowly. The balcony door remained open, sheer curtains swaying in the cool evening breeze.

Hemera sat on the floor, back resting against the sofa. Mudit sat beside her, legs stretched out, close enough for comfort but not quite touching. She held an old unlit cigarette in her hand, the one she had saved for *"Emergencies"*.

"It smells like paint," he said softly, almost to himself.

"I know," she murmured. "Even the kitchen. I keep telling myself I'll fix it, make it smell like gulab jamun or something."

He smiled faintly. "It suits you. Messy, but alive. You kinda smelled like paint in school too, back when you first joined."

She let out a quiet laugh.

"School feels like another life," she said. "Ranchi feels like another planet."

"Sometimes I still walk past your old society," he told her. "The paint's still peeling, the current guard sleeps on duty."

There was a pause. She stared ahead, eyes distant.

"It's strange," she said. "I packed everything up and left. My mother didn't follow. She didn't call. Not then, not ever."

"She hit you," Mudit said, voice low. "I remember. The bruises. The way you'd flinch when anyone raised their voice."

"Yeah." Hemera's voice cracked slightly. "But I still waited for her to say sorry. Or come after me. Isn't that stupid?"

"No," he said. "It's human."

The fan hummed gently above them. The silence between them felt tender.

"I miss Maggi," she whispered. "He is a good dog. Loyal in ways people couldn't be."

She blinked quickly, swallowing something in her throat. The wind brushed her cheek gently.

Mudit turned his head to look at her.

"I waited too," he said.

"I didn't think you would," she replied.

"Almost eight years," he said. "Through undergrad. Through med school. Everyone thought I was crazy. But I kept thinking- maybe one day you'd call. Or message. Something."

"I thought you'd moved on," she said. "Met someone?"

"No one ever made me feel the way you did," he replied. "Not once. That first time – you were painting that cracked wall during fest prep. You had purple on your cheek and didn't even care."

She laughed quietly.

"You were dissecting the fake frogs and quoting poetry. It was disgusting."

"But I loved you then," he said, eyes burning. "I still do. I don't need you to say it back. I just needed you to hear it."

Hemera turned slowly toward him, her eyes glassy but unflinching.

"I don't trust myself, Mudit," she whispered.

"That's okay," he said gently. "I'm not asking for a promise. Just. . . don't disappear again."

For a while, they said nothing.

"Okay," she finally whispered.

"Come on," Mudit smiled. "Let's get your insta set up, a famous painter like you should cultivate an online presence."

Hemera snorted, mood lightening.

"Whatever you say, doctor."

13

Thirty two year old Hemera stared at the letter in her hand.

I don't know if this will reach you. Someone from our old housing colony mentioned seeing your painting in a magazine. The one with the wildflowers and the almost empty crib with ghungroos in it. I knew it immediately. That was mine too, wasn't it?

I asked around. It took me months to find anything. Eventually, I found the name of the design studio in an article. I called. The girl on the phone said you no longer worked there, but she offered to forward a letter if I mailed it to her. I didn't mean to intrude. I just didn't know how else to reach you.

I'm writing this from a hospital bed. I won't waste your time with details, just know the doctors say it won't be long. I'm not afraid of it. Not anymore. But there are things I should've said long before this moment, and I don't want to leave without trying.

I know I was cruel to you. I know I hurt you. There are things I can't explain, only regret. I was broken in ways I didn't understand then but that's not your burden. It never should've been.

I don't ask for forgiveness, Hemera. Just- if this letter reaches you, please know that I have thought of you every single day. I know I never said the right things, but I was proud of you. I still am.

I hope you're eating well. I hope someone tells you you're good. And I hope, if you're willing, that you won't throw this letter away immediately.

On the back I have mentioned the hospital and room,

Just in case you'll come to see me.
– Ma

Hemera closed her eyes, taking a deep breath in.

She never thought she would come back to Ranchi.

Hemera ran through the hospital corridors, her slippers echoing against the sterile floors, breath caught somewhere between panic and disbelief.

At the nurses' station, a woman looked up and then stood slowly, recognition softening her expression.

"You're Ms.Vasundhara's daughter? She showed me a picture of you."

Hemera nodded frantically, "Where-"

"She passed just a few minutes ago," the nurse said gently, placing a steady hand on Hemera's arm.

But Hemera moved past her, into the room.

The air was cold. Machines silent. Her mother laid still on the narrow hospital bed, smaller than she'd remembered – gaunt, frail, and aged in a way pain does to a person. White hair had slipped from the bun she always kept so tightly pulled, and her lips were parted slightly, as if she'd been mid-sentence.

The room smelt of antiseptic.

Hemera's fingers trembled as she reached out and took her mother's hand. Cold, already beginning to stiffen. She sat beside her, eyes filling, throat burning. But she didn't shatter.

Not now.

She pressed her forehead against the back of her mother's hand, whispering into the quiet room, "Goodbye."

And then, softer, more to herself than anyone, “I would’ve come sooner, if I knew how.”

For a moment, she allowed herself to ache for her mother.

There was no last word from the woman who had once both nurtured and hurt her. No apology.

Hemera didn’t need it to survive.

14

"We'll grow old either way. I just don't want to do it without you."

Mudit turned to face her, body leaning dangerously against the railing of the balcony.

"Then stay." Hemera replied.

He smiled, a childish glint in his eyes. "Most of my stuff is already here so I would say mission accomplished."

Hemera rolled her eyes, a smile on her face.

"I know."

"Happy thirty fifth, Mera."

". . . Thank you."

Hemera's life was not loud. It didn't unfold in grand or dramatic declarations. It moved like seasons; quietly, relentlessly – with changes that only made sense in hindsight.

For years, she carried silence like a second skin, smiles over bruises that no one could see. Her childhood had taught her to flinch before reaching, to listen more than speak, and to never expect softness where duty was demanded.

She grew up watching doors slam more than they opened, her voice buried under the weight of her mother's rage and regrets. But there was always art; stolen moments with crayons and notebooks, scribbled sketches behind textbooks, and eventually, the language she used to breathe when words failed her.

Even her worst nights ended with streaks of familiar pink on paper, grief smeared into colors.

College was supposed to be freedom, and for a while, it was – the kind that came with chaos. Nights blurred with smoke and sharp-tasting drinks, with boys who smiled too easily and left even quicker. Who mirrored her ache instead of softening it. She spiraled and then stopped – not all at once, but in pieces.

A taped-up box of cigarettes, sleepless nights without giving in.

There were moments of stillness: finding herself under tropical skies, holding uneven pearls in a distant city, hearing a stranger call her *"beta"* with more love than she had thought she deserved. And there were memories she never asked for — her mother's letter, written with hands that never once held her gently, and the last breath of someone who had always left the words *"I love you"* unsaid.

Now, at thirty-five, Hemera's life grew quiet again, but in a way that feels chosen, not forced. She wakes up in a small flat filled with morning light and half-finished canvases. Mudit is beside her, steady as he had been in childhood, in grief, in love.

They still spoke of her dog Maggi, who passed away at old age happily. Of Ranchi's narrow lanes and the years that felt too long. And sometimes, Hemera touches the old pearl bracelet on her wrist and remembers: she survived. She healed.

She is still becoming.

Epilogue

On her marriage certificate, she wrote her full name for the first time in years.

Hemera Nayantara.

She had learned that life wasn't a race to escape the past – it was a quiet walk toward herself.

And she was finally home.

Acknowledgement

To those who taught me how to feel deeply, even when it hurt
– thank you.

For the last two years of my life, I've explored the themes of love, grief, and motherhood to shape this story. I had always wanted to write, to express something which I have grown to notice across every other person I have met.

This book is my labor of love, an ache in my soul which I had to spill.

I thank my parents, who have always been supportive of my dreams. My grandparents, who had lived and loved, with stories from their times. My sister, who is still growing. And my friends, who have accepted all parts of me. I thank the cities I've lived in – they've inspired and nurtured my becoming.

And to anyone who has ever tried to find their way back to themselves: this book is for you.

You were never too late.
You were always becoming.

About the Author

Pratyaksha Shukla is an up and coming author with a love for stories rooted in emotion. She first ventured into writing as a teenager, self-publishing a fantasy novel on Kindle.

Currently a student, she balances academics with her deep desire to explore human complexity through fiction. Her writing often revolves around themes of love, loss, memory, and healing – moments that shape and shift people.

She hopes to continue creating stories that hold space for feeling deeply, especially for those learning how to come home to themselves.

Join her journey: **@pratyakshawrites** on Instagram.

www.ingramcontent.com/pod-product-compliance
Ingram Content Group UK Ltd.
Pitfield, Milton Keynes, MK11 3LW, UK
UKHW041344190726
13845UKWH00026B/425

9 789334 329803